P Sivakami is a member of the Indian Administrative Service. She has published four novels and four short-story collections, and is a regular contributor to the literary magazine *Pudiya Kodangi*.

The Grip of Change
and
Author's Notes

P. SIVAKAMI

Translated from the Tamil
Pazhaiyana Kazhithalum
and
Asiriyar Kurippu
by
P. SIVAKAMI

Orient BlackSwan

ORIENT BLACKSWAN PRIVATE LIMITED

Registered Office
3-6-752, Himyatnagar, Hyderabad 500 029 (A.P), India
Email: centraloffice@orientblackswan.com

Other Offices
Bangalore, Bhopal, Bhubaneshwar, Chennai
Ernakulam, Guwahati, Hyderabad, Jaipur, Kolkata
Lucknow, Mumbai, New Delhi, Patna

First Published by Orient Longman Private Limited 2006
First Orient Blackswan Impression 2009

The Tamil original of *The Grip of Change (Pazhaiyana Kazhithalum)*
was first published in 1989 by Annam, Chennai. The Tamil original of
Author's Notes (Asiriyar Kurippu) was published in 1997 by Tamil
Puthaklayam, Chennai.

ISBN: 978 81 250 3020 1

Typeset by
Line Arts
Pondichery

Printed in India at
Novena Offset
Chennai 600 005

Published by
Orient Blackswan Private Limited
160, Annasalai, Chennai 600 002
Email: chennai@orientblackswan.com

CONTENTS

PREFACE

I am one of the many exploring the inexhaustible mysteries of caste; of course, in my own way. To me, writing still remains a process of understanding and sharing. This process has seldom extinguished the desire to move events to their logical conclusion, and the desire for ·philosphical progression. From there, the journey begins again.

I wrote the Tamil novel, *Pazhaiyana Kazhithalum*, when I was twenty-six. But when I read it later, I found that my expressions were limited to that of a seventeen-year-old girl. Perhaps due to the fact that I could not stretch myself to the distant past with ease and fluency, and the present proved to be tough meat to chew.

After about ten years, I went back to my novel as a third person, with the hope that I could see the author more objectively. The second book, *Asiriyar Kurippu*, is the result of such an attempt. To my surprise, in spite of my efforts to analyse the novel critically, I found that I had actually ended up justifying my views. Thus the novel, *The Grip of Change*, is a process of understanding the dynamics of caste and the 'woman' who was inextricably involved in the process.

What have I understood?

That it is natural for me as a Dalit and a woman – factors decided by birth – to write about those factors. And thereby I firmly place myself within a circle, influencing the politics surrounding those factors.

I understand that it is the need of the hour and the requirement of the future.

I also understand that I need to continue with my efforts not only in creative writing but also in other spheres.

I am glad that I could translate this into English for a wider readership. I thank my friend Vivienne Kenrick, and R. Sivapriya of Orient Longman, who have helped me greatly with the translation. I thank S. Anand for helping my manuscript find a publisher. I thank C.S. Lakshmi and Meena Kandasamy for contributing their readings.

P. Sivakami
Chennai
October 2005

BOOK ONE

KATHAMUTHU
THE GRIP OF CHANGE

ONE

Kathamuthu woke up at four in the morning even as the first streaks of dawn were lighting the sky. He slid his wife's hand away from his chest, and yawned and stretched. Nagamani, the second wife he had installed in his home, was moaning in her sleep as if she were in pain. Her skirt loosened, curly hair dishevelled, eyes only half closed, she seemed determined to stay asleep. Her sari had floated down to a corner of the room and fluttered each time the breeze from the fan caught it.

Kathamuthu arose and checked his veshti for the right side, and tied it around his waist. He picked up the sari from the corner and tossed it over Nagamani.

'Cover yourself. I'm leaving.' Without waiting for an answer, he unlatched the door, went out into the hall, and peered through the window into the next room. His first wife Kanagavalli was fast asleep. She was holding Sekaran, the younger child, tight. The older child, Gowri, lay clinging to her mother's back.

'She's a grown-up now, but sleeps clinging to her mother, like an infant,' he thought as he opened the outside door and, startled, stopped abruptly. Something dark loomed in the corner of the verandah. Slowly, as Kathamuthu's eyes grew accustomed to the shadows, he could make out a person crouching there, groaning in pain.

'Who is it? What…?' Kathamuthu asked fearfully.

'Ayyo…Ayyo…They have butchered me…Ayyo…' The figure cried like a wounded animal and finally fell down.

Unexpected commotion in the quiet of the morning disturbed the family inside. Behind him, Kathamuthu heard the women call

and come running. Gowri, frightened, began to wail. Nagamani
rushed out, bunching up her sari. Kanagavalli too hurried out.

Panic stricken they asked, 'What happened? What happened?'

They calmed down on seeing Kathamuthu frozen at the entrance.

'You woman…you…why are you here wailing so early in
the morning? What is the matter? Get up and explain your
problem without making such a fuss.' Flanked by both his wives,
Kathamuthu recovered from the shock he had experienced and
questioned the shrouded figure.

'What can I say? May they be hanged. May they go to hell. The
ground will open up and swallow you. You'll eat mud. Bastards!
You abused a helpless woman. You curs! Come now! Come and
lick…'

What should have been an explanation turned into a torrent of
abuse against those who had assaulted her. She seemed to be
seeing their figures in front of her.

'Shut up, bitch. Don't you dare use foul language here. I'll hit
your mouth. Don't you have any respect for the man you're talking
to? If you've nothing more to say, piss off.' Kathamuthu spoke in
anger and irritation.

'My saviour! Sami! To whom can I tell this, but you? That's why
I came running all that distance, all through the night, to see you.
See what those rascals did to me.'

Weeping, she removed the sari wrapped around her head. The
whole of her torso, visible because she was not wearing a blouse,
bore terrible bruises. Dried blood marked the flesh of her back.

'Ayyo…Sivane!' Nagamani exclaimed at the injuries.

'Who did this to you?' Kanagavalli wondered. Gowri looked at
the woman, full of fear and pity. The raw wounds made Sekaran
close his eyes.

'Sami. Not only this, Sami. Look at my arms.' She showed her
swollen arms.

'Look at this Sami.' The woman lifted her sari above her knees.

'Oh! Ayyo!'

The skin of her thighs and knees was scored and shredded as though she had been dragged over a rough surface.

Kathamuthu, who had maintained a stunned silence so far, asked in the businesslike tone of someone who had once been the elected president of the panchayat council, 'Where are you from? What is your caste? And your name?'

'Sami, these hooligans who beat me up, they should be jailed for at least a day and tortured. The pain is killing me.'

'Don't tell me what I should do. Answer my questions first.' She seemed unable to reply coherently. Impatient, he turned around and began to allocate work to each member of his family. 'Nagu, get some hot water and clean those wounds. Sekar, run to Muchamy vaidyar. Drag him here, if you have to. While you're at it, buy milk on your way back. Gowri, why are you standing there doing nothing? Clean the front yard and spray the cow dung.'

Sekaran, pulling up his shorts with one hand and holding the bronze pot for the milk in the other, bolted out.

As if becoming aware of the movement around her, the woman stopped crying. She blew her nose with her fingers and wiped them on the wall.

Kathamuthu took her to be in her thirties, tall and well built. Though her face was swollen from crying, it was still attractive. He leaned back against the wall, rolled his veshti into a parcel between his legs and sat down.

'Sami, I come from the same village as your wife Kanagavalli. Kanagu, don't you recognise me? You know Kaipillai from the south street who died? I am his wife.'

'Oh! Oh yes. My god, it is you! Why did they beat you up so badly? I didn't recognise you with your head covered. My god!'

'Oh, where shall I begin? You know Paranjothi from the upper caste street?' she appealed to Kanagu.

'I don't know anyone from the upper caste locality. I was very young when I got married and since then I've hardly been to the village. Even if I have to go, I only visit my family. And I never step outside our street. The bus stops at the irrigation tank, and there's never any need to go further.'

'True. People like you living in towns don't know much about villages.' She swallowed hard, 'Paranjothi from the upper caste street is very rich. His lands go right up to the next village, Arumadal. After my husband died I began working in Paranjothi's farm. My husband's brothers refused to hand over his share of the family land as I didn't have any children. How could I fight them? I couldn't go to court. Who can spend that much money? Even if I had won, I wouldn't be able to take care of my share of land in peace, not with everyone hating me. I am a single woman now. But Munusamy, the god on the mountain, is watching. One day he will take their measure. I am a poor widow. But at least I have a thatched roof over my head.

'My husband's relatives spread the story that I had become Paranjothi's concubine. That's why Paranjothi's wife's brothers and her brother-in-law, four men, entered my house last night. They pulled me by my hair and dragged me out to the street. They hit me, and flogged me with a stick stout as a hand. They nearly killed me. No one in the village, none of my relatives, came to help me. I begged for mercy, but they wouldn't stop. They abused me and threatened to kill me if I stayed in that village any longer. They called me a whore.' She began to wail again.

'Okay, okay.' Kathamuthu studied her, 'Now tell me the truth. What did you do? Nobody would have assaulted you like that unless you had done something first.'

'I didn't do anything wrong. I didn't throw mud on anyone's food,' she sobbed without hope.

'That's enough. Take your story to someone else who might be fool enough to believe it.' Kathamuthu sounded determined to get the truth from her.

Kanagu intervened, 'Tell him what happened, as it happened. Then he'll know what to do without causing you any harm.'

'Ayya, you are all gods to me. How can I hide the truth from you? Paranjothi Udayar has had me...true,' she said, her expression a mixture of fear and shame.

'Why do you have to spoil someone's marriage? Is that good? You've hurt his family,' Kanagavalli stressed the last part for the benefit of Nagamani who had come to the verandah with the hot water. Nagamani directed a scornful look at Kathamuthu.

Quick to take the hint, Kathamuthu rounded on Kanagavalli, 'Are you here to pass judgement early in the morning? Go inside and get some coffee. Now!'

'Everyone laughs at the set-up in your home, and here you are trying to teach others. You think you are such a bigshot!' Kanagavalli went inside, muttering so that he could hear.

The woman, though a little confused, had grasped the situation, 'Sami, is there anywhere on earth where this doesn't happen? I didn't want it. But Udayar took no notice of me. He raped me when I was working in his sugarcane field. I remained silent, after all, he is my paymaster. He measures my rice. If you think I'm like that, that I'm easy, please ask around in the village. After my husband's death, can anybody say that they had seen me in the company of anyone, or even smiling at anyone? My husband's brothers tried to force me, but I never gave in. They wouldn't give me my husband's land, but wanted me to be a whore for them! I wouldn't give in. Each time one of them came near me I brandished the broom. After that none of them came anywhere near me. I am a childless widow. There is no protection for me.'

Kathamuthu interrupted her, 'All right, it happened. Now tell me, why didn't you go after someone of our caste? It's because you chose that upper caste fellow, that four men could come and righteously beat you up. Don't you like our chaps?'

Hesitating at the crudity of his remarks, she answered, 'Sami, how can you ask me such a question? I didn't go after anyone. I am not a desperate woman. I feel so ashamed. It was wrong, horrible...

I gave in to Udayar…You should abandon me in some jungle, I never want to go back to that village. But before that I want those men who beat me up to fall at my feet and plead.' She angrily grabbed some mud from the front yard and spat on it.

She raised her hands as if to pray, but instead wrung them. After a minute she said, 'Sami, if you think it was my fault, hit me with your slippers.' She began beating her chest with both hands, until she fell on the floor, almost unconscious.

Nagamani who was standing nearby, with the hot water now forgotten, felt tears pour down her cheeks.

'You don't have to hurt her any more, talking like that. That's the difference between the educated and the uneducated.' She knelt to attend to the woman.

The woman let Nagamani clean her wounds without fully regaining consciousness.

Nagamani queried anxiously, 'We shouldn't keep her here any longer. She ought to be taken to a hospital.'

'She has to be hospitalised. Muchamy should see her before that. An FIR has to be registered against those who beat her. She has to write a complaint.' Kathamuthu made a list of tasks, lost in thought.

As Kathamuthu was speaking, Muchamy vaidyar and Sekaran had arrived. It was five thirty in the morning, and the sun was steadily climbing up the sky. Sekaran handed the pot of milk to his mother and ran back to the verandah to watch Muchamy examine the woman.

'I have made the coffee,' said Kanagavalli, thumping a large container of coffee on the floor. Gowri brought the stainless steel tumblers that she had just washed. Kanagavalli poured coffee for everyone, setting a tumbler aside for the doctor and another for the woman.

Perhaps Kathamuthu felt a twinge of conscience at his gruffness. He softened the tone in which he spoke to the woman, quietened by the doctor's touch.

'Look here. What's your name?'

'My name is Thangam, Sami.'

'Oh, "Gold"! The broomstick is tied with a silk thread.' Proud of his little joke, Kathamuthu winked at Nagamani.

'That's only to be expected of you,' she said, sneering at him. 'The frog asks for trouble with its own voice, doesn't it? That proverb is one hundred per cent true in your case. Had you not always indulged in cheap jokes at others' expense, you would have become a member of parliament by now. You never behave with the dignity appropriate for a man of stature.'

Kathamuthu growled at her in annoyance, 'What are you muttering about now? You said I should have been educated, and now you're saying I'm not dignified. Shut your mouth! Nobody cared for you till I took you into my house. And she says that the whole town is laughing at me. What do you both think? I'll tear you to pieces!'

'Come on, let's go in. We have nothing to do here,' Kanagavalli said to Nagamani. They picked up their coffee and went in.

Muchamy, having finished checking the patient, straightened his frail body, 'She'll have to go to the hospital. But here's an ointment, and give her these tablets.'

'All right,' Kathamuthu snapped. 'You don't have to wait. I'll send your payment through Sekar.' Disappointed, but careful not to show his feelings, Muchamy left.

Gowri, leaning against the wall, kept her eyes on her short-tempered father. She was scared of him. She never brought any of her friends home, though she would have liked to show them her love-birds, and the beautiful back garden where the samandis were in full bloom. She was always afraid that he would fly into a rage for no reason in front of her friends.

'You lazy girl! What are you staring at? Run and get pen and paper. I'd like to know what you learn in school. You go there in full make-up like a movie extra, a cartload of that black stuff on your eyes, ashamed of carrying a sack of rice on your head just as far as the mill. Hmm…Is that what education teaches you? You're afraid of your friends seeing you with a bag of rice on your head? You'd better go and live with them. They'll fill your stomach. All because of the wretched cinema…' Kathamuthu scolded incoherently.

'Paper, pen…' Gowri raced back with what he wanted in order to stop him from carrying on further. He looked her up and down, and took the writing material from her with deliberate slowness.

Thangam, caught between the tension created by Kathamuthu and her aching body, sat whimpering.

He cleared his throat importantly, spat, and turned his attention to the woman.

'Look, I'll be straight with you, even if I sound rude. I'm living with this woman who doesn't belong to our community. She's upper caste. She was a struggling widow, so I provided her a safe haven.'

Gowri squirming at her father's story, quietly slipped away. Kathamuthu went on, 'Why should I bother with this story? Okay, I liked her, and she was willing. And now she lives like a queen. I'm a man with some say in the community, as you know, once even elected president of the panchayat. No one can question me. But your case is different. You are a woman. Upper caste men may fancy you, but they'll not marry you. You won't even be able to step into their houses. Well, there may be some rare exceptions and you may get to spend your life as a concubine. But tell me, why did they beat you up? Because you are lower caste, that's why. For all that's happened, Udayar has stayed out of it, hasn't he? That's why I said you should have chosen one of our men.'

Tears rolling down her cheeks, Thangam remained silent. As she slowly understood the abuses she had been subjected to, she felt miserable. The memories made her sob in distress,

'Stop your snivelling now. Tell me the names of those men and we'll lodge a complaint with the police. There's no use howling. Gowri, come here,' Kathamuthu summoned his daughter.

The frown on Gowri's face infuriated Kathamuthu. He raised his voice, 'Write what I say. Write it clearly, understand?'

Without looking at him, Gowri sat on the floor. She placed her elbow on the paper, and propped her face on her left hand.

Katahmuthu began to dictate.

'In the said zila...said taluk...said village...what's your father's name?'

Thangam, watching Gowri and unprepared for the abrupt question directed at her, stumbled. 'My father's name is Paramasivam.'

'You don't know your own father's name? Strange...,' Kathamuthu leered. 'What have you written, girl?'

'In the said district...said circle...said village...' Gowri watched her father's face as she read aloud. She enjoyed having her slight revenge on him, drawing attention to his outdated language.

He smiled to himself at her changing of the words. 'She's smart. She'll survive,' he thought to himself approvingly.

'Thangam, daughter of the late Paramasivam and wife of the late Kaipillai, petitions her poor orphan's complaint.'

Gowri wrote 'deceased' in place of 'late', and glowed at the change.

'Gowri, begin with "To the respected Inspector of Police" at the top.'

'Over,' she answered, feeling like a professional writer of petitions sitting in the sub-magistrate's court.

'Right. Continue. I belong to the Hindu Scheduled Caste community. I am a poor Parayar, an orphan, a widow. I earn my living by working for a daily wage. On the night of the event, I was passing along the upper caste street to attend to a call of nature. At that time, Paranjothi Udayar's wife...what's her name?'

'Kamalam.'

'Udayar's wife Kamalam glared at me scornfully, and shouted, "You Paraya bitch, how dare you walk on this street? Is this not the upper caste street? Go away from here."' Gowri stopped writing and looked at her father enquiringly.

'Why have you stopped? Write as I say. You can't change anything here as you changed zila to district. There is a reason for presenting it this way,' he responded arrogantly.

He repeated, '"Why is the Paraya bitch walking along this street? Don't you know it is an upper caste street? Go away from here," said Kamalam.'

'That's finished. No need to go over it.' Gowri's dislike of any mention of caste sharpened her voice.

'And there's no need for you to bark like a dog,' he snapped, and carried on.

Gowri continued to write with tears stinging her eyes.

'I replied to Kamalam, "Amma, this road is laid by the government, and you can't order me away." Kamalam reacted like a wild animal when I answered her. She insulted me and my caste. Again I told her politely, "Amma, why do you abuse me like that?" She replied, "Yes, I will abuse you, and you'd tear me apart if you could, wouldn't you?" I asked her again not to talk like that. But she lunged at me and said, "Are you threatening me, you low caste bitch?" and picked up a thick stick and began to beat me. I tried to run away but her brothers – what are their names? – her brothers Subbu Udayar, Manicka Udayar and Mayilvahana Udayar, and the said Kamalam's brother-in-law Perumal Udayar—all four pulled me by my hair, tore my blouse, beat my breasts, dragged me along the street naked and tried to murder me...'

Kathamuthu looked at Thangam and asked, 'Isn't that right?'

'Yes. They did all that. Everything is true. But it wasn't in the upper caste street. It was in our street, and in front of my house.'

Her naivety infuriated Kathamuthu. 'You are such a stupid bitch. I've changed the whole story. Don't you understand? Now don't screw it up. If you say anything different from what's written in the petition, you'll be jailed. Understand?'

Thangam nodded. Gowri uneasy at what was going on, wondered why her father was the way he was.

TWO

By seven o'clock, the sun was high in a cloudless sky. Grumbling, Kathamuthu walked to the back yard. He filled an iron pail with water, and carried it to the red-tiled toilet.

'Which idiot has done this? Sekar, will you never wash the toilet after you use it?' he fumed. He emptied the pail into the toilet, splashing the water freely. He went out to get some more water. It was another fifteen minutes by the time he came out, muttering and cursing.

'Hopeless bastards. Nothing to eat. Yet they have all the pride in the world...' Abusing someone with choice expletives, he stomped around to the front of the house. Thangam lay curled up on the verandah. He felt a pang of pity for her as he went up to get *Dinamani*, rolled up and tucked between the bars of the iron gate. He went back with it to his chair on the verandah and settled down.

Scratching his head, hesitant, Subramani appeared at the gate. He had appointed himself as an assistant to Kathamuthu, hoping to get a job through him at the taluk office. Subramani had failed his school final examinations and did not know what to do. He had no money to set up even a small business for himself, and he didn't want to labour on the land. A menial government job or even one in a private company would do. By attaching himself to Kathamuthu, he hoped to find a way to earn his living.

Kathamuthu saw him shuffling at the gate and lowered his newspaper. 'Good. You're on time. I want you to take this woman to the government hospital. Mention my name to the doctor. I'll take care of the rest later, okay? After that bring her to the police station around eleven thirty. I'll be there waiting for you.'

Kathamuthu went inside, leaving Subramani to carry out his orders.

Subramani helped Thangam get up. He saw the bus for Athur coming and ran to stop it. It would pass by the government hospital.

Gowri was plucking flowers from the jasmine creeper covering the compound wall. She kept stealing glances at Thangam. 'I belong to the same caste as that woman. How can I be sure that I won't be beaten black and blue like her? I have seen things like this happening in the cinema. This is real, terror is sleeping on a mat in my house.' She felt revulsion for the society where such things could happen. Her thoughts chilled her, even as the morning grew hot. 'I must run off to school before he finishes his bath. If he sees me, he'll yell at me for wearing flowers on my hair, kohl in my eyes, and even the pottu on my brow for that matter.'

Water overflowed from the outdoor cement water-tub and made its way through the coconut grove. More water spilled out, drenching the samandis, as Kathamuthu got into the tub. Stepping out after his bath, he wrapped the wet towel around his waist, faced the sun, and folded his hands. He began reciting the taraka mantram to seduce the Devi. 'Om Sarvasoosari, Sankari, Chamundi, Rubi—destroyer of Taraka, protector of the devas...'

Lately, after his bath, he had taken to chanting this mantram, a practice he had picked up from Vakil Venkatakrishnan, a Brahmin lawyer. Using three fingers, he took thiruneer from a wooden box and applied it on his forehead in three broad strokes.

When he sat down for breakfast, as he scooped up some chutney with a piece of idli, he remembered Thangam. He called out to the kitchen, 'Oh, I'd forgotten, did you give that woman something to eat?'

'We gave her breakfast a long while ago. Nobody here is waiting for your orders,' Kanagavalli replied.

'Good. Poor wretch! Now I can eat.'

He called out again, 'Gowri, Gowri. Where are you? Not going to school?'

'She left ten minutes ago.'

'Left already? With her hair full of flowers, no doubt. Well, as long as she works hard...'

He tipped some water on to his plate and dabbed his fingers in it. 'I have to go to the court. I'll be back for lunch.'

THREE

Kathamuthu was aware that he looked good, his spotless white veshti and shirt contrasting well with his healthy dark skin glowing from the bath. He had earned the reputation of being a good man. But those who praised him also added that he always had too much to say and was also arrogant. He was like an itchy pig, never keeping still. Everyone knew he was always out and about, not a person who indulged himself in rest and leisure. He knew he was a man of consequence—a popular, respected leader of the people of Athur and the nearby villages. He had made it his career to help people in distress. He didn't have much land, and its yield was average, but he could never pay enough attention to cultivating his own holding while he was busy sorting out village affairs. People depended on him because he never gave up. He was completely unafraid of anyone or anything. Humility and restraint were non-existent words in the vocabulary of this domineering man. He justified everything that he did with an inexhaustible source of stories from the Mahabharata and the Ramayana. His daughter Gowri was inclined to occasionally dip into the two epics because of this.

Kathamuthu's household was like any other with two wives—haunted by petty quarrels and bickering. In the beginning, when Nagamani moved in, every day there would be arguments between him and Kanagavalli, and between the two women. After each quarrel there would be an uneasy silence until some fresh squabble broke out. Gowri and Sekaran would hide themselves. When Nagamani had first come, she had brought practically nothing with her, not even a change of sari. She had had a hard time after her husband's death. At a time when she had been disillusioned with family and community, she had settled for Kathamuthu, though of a lower caste, then a young panchayat president who had befriended her. She had learned to disregard his painful sarcasm and had adjusted well to her new life in his home. In fact, Kanagavalli and her children now provided solace to her. There were still occasional quarrels, but they blew over quickly. While amicably weeding the plaintain grove or making brooms out of coconut palms in each other's company, their conversation ranged on the ways of the world.

Kathamuthu was often surprised, and at times felt uneasy. At first, when he called them to press his legs, they would shove each other out of the way, literally pulling each other's hair to get to him first. But now – alas! – even after he called out several times one of them would appear unwillingly as if she had lost out to the other. And this morning, after laying out the breakfast, they had disappeared into the kitchen, not bothering to wait on him, talking to each other in hushed tones. Kathamuthu thought this over while walking down the dusty, noisy road. 'Those two have ganged up on me. If this continues, I'll have to bring another woman home!' The thought made him smile.

'Laughing to yourself, Mama?' Rangasamy's voice brought him back.

'I am now related even to beggars, am I?' Kathamuthu laughed aloud, revealing his dazzling white teeth.

'Yes, I am a poor beggar. Why don't you feed me tonight?'

'Dei, you'll test the teeth of the cow offered for free. Your mother's labour has filled my house with coconuts in one corner and mangoes in the other. Of course, you can feast off them,' he retorted, mussing the makeshift turban on Rangasamy's head.

'Mama, you have taken my turban?'

'Behave respectfully, wear it on your shoulder.'

'Can I afford to wear white and white like you? I'm not swindling the village.' Seeing the look on Kathamuthu's face, Rangasamy realised he'd gone too far.

'You rascal! Get going! Fuck off, I say,' Kathamuthu shouted, raising his hand as if to strike Rangasamy.

'Mama, I was just joking.'

Kathamuthu lowered his hand and walked away.

'He was joking? I do all I can for my community, but they show me no respect. Look at them! Even if they starve, they can't stop teasing people. I treat everyone as an equal, and then I end up being insulted!'

Worried by the unexpected turn his joke had taken, Rangasamy stood staring at Kathamuthu's departing back. Remembering his lack of a steady job, he felt a stab of fear. He stood rooted to the spot for a long time, anxious and tearful. He decided to beg Kathamuthu's forgiveness that evening.

Distantly related to Kathamuthu, Rangasamy was an agricultural labourer. On most days, he worked on Kathamuthu's land, thus earning his daily wage. He would also get lunch, and in the evenings a tumbler of arrack, if Kathamuthu was in a good mood. Hoping that he would be forgiven if he requested Kanagavalli for some work in the plaintain grove, Rangasamy hurried towards Kathamuthu's house.

Kathamuthu walked fast, keeping his eyes down, hoping to avoid any further encounters. His irritation with Rangasamy kept him silent on his way to the police station. He could not ignore some important people, to them he said, 'I'm going to the police station, I am in a hurry,' and kept going. Nothing seemed to be going right since morning. Kathamuthu felt that it was not a good day for him.

The police station was in an ugly red-painted building. The deep blue flowers blooming around the compound were coated with the dust from the road. Small coffee stalls lined the street. Opposite the police station was Naicker's jewellery shop. Naicker was hoping to find a different location for his shop. The small bribes that he had to frequently pay the policemen, to keep them from troubling him, were proving to be ruinous.

Kathamuthu was obliged to greet Naicker who was standing outside his shop. He shouted to be heard above the noise of the street, 'Vanakkam Naicker!'

'What brings you here? Why don't you come in,' Naicker shouted back.

'I have work to do. Keeping you company won't help get the work done.'

'Come on, you can have coffee and then do a good day's work.'

Naicker had not seen Kathamuthu for some time and was keen to have a chat on what was a slow day for him. Naicker always enjoyed Kathamuthu's talk, spiced as it was with coarseness. Kathamuthu could brighten any dull subject with his picturesque language. Naicker could not use the crude phrases that Kathamuthu could get away with, and was always entertained by them. After Kathamuthu left his shop, Naicker invariably commented to others, 'Poor fellow, he belongs to a lower caste. Can't you tell from his gross speech?'

Somebody had once repeated Naicker's remark to Kathamuthu. Kathamuthu had reacted by snubbing the tale-teller, 'Yes, he speaks the truth, I belong to a lower caste. So what?' After that, he let Naicker know that his remarks had been reported back to Kathamuthu. Naicker's apologies could not win Kathamuthu over.

'Kathamuthu, if I have offended you, why don't you abuse me as "brutish Naicker"?'

'"Brutish Naicker"! Is that an abuse at all? I'll get back at you some time, you bastard.' Kathamuthu left it at that for the time being.

As a result, Naicker added to his usual comment on Kathamuthu's caste, 'Don't tell him I called him lower caste. He'll come to my store and make a song and dance about it.'

Kathamuthu got his revenge a little later, when his relative from a remote village came to Naicker's jewellery shop to buy silver araignan for his newborn baby. Naicker kept him standing, and carefully dropped the silver piece on his palm from a distance in order to avoid touching him. The relative had promptly complained to Kathamuthu.

The following day, Kathamuthu showed up at Naicker's store. Naicker could tell at once that something was wrong, even before Kathamuthu began railing at him.

'If I ever come to your store again, slap me with your chappal. I'm never going to cross your threshold again.'

'Why don't you sit? What's wrong?' Naicker put his hand on Kathamuthu's shoulder.

'Why are you touching me Naicker? Isn't it a sin if you touch me?' asked Kathamuthu provocatively.

'I don't understand. Look, Kathamuthu. Was it what I said? You know I never pay any attention to caste. I am not a Brahmin preserving the old order, afraid of the wrath of the gods. All that I am particular about is cleanliness. That's all.'

His attitude angered Kathamuthu further.

'Oho, so there is another meaning to untouchability. I didn't know that. Right, don't you come near me with your foul breath and stained teeth. You talk about cleanliness. Just you look at my teeth.' His teeth were indeed admirable and his gums a healthy pink.

Naicker was deeply affronted, but put on a smile. He had of course noticed that his wife moved away whenever he attempted to go near her.

'Cleanliness! Our chaps toil in the mud every day, worse than cattle. If you gave them enough money, you'd be surprised to see how handsome they could be. Cleanliness!'

However, their relationship continued. Kathamuthu sometimes had to borrow money from Naicker. On his part, Naicker sometimes wanted Kathamuthu's help in government- or court-related matters. In Naicker's eyes, Kathamuthu was a necessary evil.

When Naicker invited him in, Kathamuthu could not refuse to go in, but he did not stay either. He went up the steps, told Naicker about the case and promised to be back later. Naicker set aside five rupees to entertain Kathamuthu later with coffee.

At the police station, the constable at the door saluted Kathamuthu. Kathamuthu leaned close to ask, 'Is the boss in?'

'Yes. But he's in a foul mood,' forewarned the constable.

Kathamuthu looked around for Subramani and Thangam. What had happened to the two of them? Why couldn't they be on time? He walked around the station to kill time. When they showed up, Kathamuthu launched into Subramani viciously.

'Why are you so late? You jobless fellow, how the fuck are you going to do a government job if you can't be on time?' He cut short Subramani's stammered explanation with, 'Don't give me any stories.'

Kathamuthu turned to the woman and asked, 'Did they give you some medicine?'

'Yes. But the pain is terrible.' She displayed the bandages to him.

Taken aback by her answer to a rhetorical question, Kathamuthu mumbled, 'Yes, well, injuries are meant to cause pain. They're not for pleasure.' He looked around and took her to a tree-shaded corner to instruct her.

'Listen. As soon as we go in, you must fall at the feet of the inspector and cry as you did this morning at my house. Understand? Don't answer any of his questions on your own. He can trap you. Tell him "Ayya will tell you everything." Then I'll take over.' Kathamuthu knew the procedure usually followed by poor plaintiffs at the police station.

As they stepped in, the head constable, his cap off, was sitting at a table inside the police station. He and Kathamuthu greeted each other. Thinking the head constable was the inspector, Thangam fell at his feet under the table, and began screaming at the top of her voice. 'Ayyo! Ayyo!' Her swollen and streaming eyes authenticated her screams.

Well, he was the head constable, Kathamuthu said to himself. Her naivety was touching. Aloud, in a kind voice, he said, 'Come,' and bent to help her up and lead her to the inspector's office.

The inspector received them affably. Privately he was wondering what sort of a day he was in for, and wished he had gone off on a tour.

Thangam did not fall at the inspector's feet. Kathamuthu had not asked her to do that twice. She was both scared and confused. Kathamuthu signalled her, but she did not understand and just stared at the inspector. Hugely irritated, Kathamuthu had to instruct her aloud, 'Please give your petition as you prostrate yourself at your saviour's feet.'

Mechanically she obeyed. She went down on the floor in the way she did before Udayar, when he handed out inexpensive saris to his employees on Deepavali or Pongal. Her lack-lustre performance grated on Kathamuthu.

The inspector did not want the woman at his feet with Kathamuthu present. He got up quickly to divert her. 'I heard you wailing outside. There's no need to carry on like that in a police station. Tell me briefly what you have to say.'

Thangam looked at Kathamuthu pathetically. Happy that the inspector had heard Thangam, Kathamuthu told her to show the bandages. Thangam showed them, her face bruised and sorrowful.

The inspector glanced at the petition in his hand and said, 'All right. I'll take care of this.'

'Ayya, if you can tell us what exactly you will do…' Kathamuthu stopped short of completing his sentence. The inspector's response was not good enough for him.

'The usual. I'll make enquiries.'

'Please don't stop with enquiries. May I say something?'

The inspector looked at him questioningly.

'You have been here only a year. I was born and brought up here, I have planted seed and ate the fruit as well. I know these villages and the people intimately. The Puliyur Udayars are stinking rich. They can buy anybody. They have beaten up this poor, lonely, lower caste woman, and they think they can get away with it. That has always been the case with those upper caste fellows. Unfortunately, there is no unity amongst the lower castes. I include myself too. They are afraid of the rich upper castes. If the lower caste people were united, do you think that Udayar's men could beat her up like this? I know you are upper caste yourself. Personally I respect the upper castes. They are educated and god-fearing. I have confidence in you. You will not be prejudiced because of caste.' He stopped to gauge whether his speech was having any effect.

The inspector responded sharply, 'Don't bring up the question of caste. I told you, I'll do the needful.'

Kathamuthu sensed that the inspector was keen to get rid of him. He switched tactics, 'I hope I haven't annoyed you, but tell me a place where caste doesn't exist. Just because you and I don't talk about it, doesn't mean it's not there. It will persist till you and I die. In fact, caste will be around for generations yet to come. We can't ignore it.'

'Is there any necessity for you to give me a lecture on caste? I've promised you that I'll take action.'

'Sir, I am not educated like you. I have just studied till class three. Thereafter my mother had to leave me as a bonded labourer in an upper caste household. I tended their cattle. By god's grace, I am in a good position now. But you know, my own people couldn't bear to see me successful. Otherwise, I would have been a member of the legislative assembly. They only vote for those who pay...'

He realised that he had strayed from the subject. He asked the inspector to be patient with him. 'Sir, what I want to make clear is that, since you are upper caste, if you don't book the culprits, people may accuse you of being biased. That could be bad for your career. That worries me.'

Evidently he had touched a nerve. The inspector who had remained unmoved by praise became flushed with anger. In the presence of Kathamuthu he called the head constable and ordered him to open an enquiry immediately. If investigations proved that Thangam's complaint was true, he ordered them to prepare an arrest warrant and bring in the accused men.

Kathamuthu chuckled to himself and lied aloud, 'In all my life, I have never come across such a dutiful and straightforward officer as you.' Having pleased the inspector with his lavish flattery, he beckoned to Thangam, 'Come, we should be leaving.' He strode ahead, asking Subramani to bring Thangam to Naicker's shop.

'Well, well, Kathamuthu seems happy,' marvelled Naicker. 'Success?'

'Almost. How about tea, pakoda and mixture for all of us?'

'It seems you've decided to loot my shop.' Naicker surreptitiously exchanged the five-rupee note for a ten-rupee note. 'Make sure the tea's piping hot,' he instructed his shop assistant.

'Come in, don't be afraid. Sit there,' Naicker invited Thangam and Subramani into his shop. Snacks and tea were partaken. As a few customers drifted in, Thangam got up.

'Yes, it's time for you to leave.' Kathamuthu turned to Naicker, 'Can you spare twenty rupees for her, in case she needs something.'

'Don't put it into your own pocket,' said Naicker, giving Kathamuthu two ten-rupee notes.

'Don't give the money to me. Give it to her. Eh, come and take it. Subramani, leave her at the hospital, I'll send someone there later, and you come home for your meal tonight.'

On his way out, Kathamuthu quipped to Naicker, 'Why do you make a fuss over just twenty rupees?'

'What? Why couldn't you give her the money yourself?'

'Where from? I don't have that kind of money from a sugar-cane field to pour into a jewellery shop.'

'Yes. Money pours down and you shower it on passers-by.'

Kathamuthu took leave, 'You and your family will be blessed for giving money to that poor woman.'

Miffed at the loss of thirty rupees, Naicker assuaged himself by cursing Kathamuthu, 'Lower caste bastard!'

The cloudless sky resembled a harvested field—bare and desolate. Only the mid-day sun burned, like a lonely child crying for water in the middle of the field. The snacks in Naicker's shop had taken the edge off Kathamuthu's appetite, but he thought he'd be ready for lunch by the time he reached home. He walked briskly to induce hunger, recognising the irony of his action in a country full of people with no means to satisfy their hunger. Desultory thoughts raced along with him. He went straight to the back yard to wash his feet before entering the house.

'Who's there?' Nagamani called out.

Not answering, he went into the kitchen to surprise her.

'Did you expect somebody else?'

'Why don't you hold a lamp and keep watch?' said Nagamani as she placed the food before him.

'Where is she?'

'Who?'

'She.'

'She?

'Is there anyone other than her in the house?'

'May be. Who knows?'

'Don't be cheeky. Do you think I can't get another woman? I still have the ability to do so.'

'That kind of ability should be beaten with a chappal—not once, but five times.'

Kanagavalli had come in from somewhere, and she and Nagamani chorused their retorts to Kathamuthu.

'Oh, you are here too. You are both monsters. Don't attack me now!' He raised his arms playfully to fend himself.

As he washed his hands he queried, 'Now, who is going to press my feet?'

Nagamani retorted, 'When one has a headache, the old woman asks for a partner to help her pound the grain! Do you realise we haven't eaten yet?'

'Come after you've eaten.'

'What about you massaging my aching head? It's been hurting all day. Then I'll come and press your legs,' Kanagavalli offered.

'Oho, is that the way this is going?' Kathamuthu hummed a song from a film. Something about 'Time has changed...god's to blame.' Humming he went to his room to pick up the newspaper where he'd left it.

FOUR

The village of Puliyur must have derived its name from the abundant tamarind trees surrounding it. In the month of Chittirai, the flat, sour fruits, delicate shelled, were always plentiful. The lime-green leaves in Aavani after the summer rains were especially beautiful. In Puliyur, the village and the cheri were almost joined. Perhaps it was those few tamarind trees positioned in between them that kept them apart.*

---

* The Dalit communities are confined to the cheri, a ghetto located at the margins of the village. The village or gramam is that part where the caste Hindus live. The term village in the Tamil context denotes both the exclusive habitation of the caste Hindus and the combined settlements of all castes—touchable and untouchable.

That day, the Mariamman temple at the centre of the Puliyur cheri was crowded and noisy with most of the residents assembled there. Many of them, especially the younger ones, seemed unusually excited. The atmosphere was crackling with tension. For upper caste men to enter into the cheri and assault a woman – however much she might be in the wrong – was unacceptable. The episode had left the residents of the cheri angry and tense. With only about two hundred households in the cheri, such an affair could not be overlooked. People wanted to hear about it from Thangam herself.

But then...

The previous night, when most people had retired into their homes for their evening meal, and some had already fallen asleep, the screams from that lonely corner hut had disturbed the cheri. But by the time people had bustled out to check what was happening, a woman was being dragged on to the road. Seeing people arriving from all sides, the assailants had yelled threats at them. Then they had run out of the cheri to the upper caste part of the village through the Chakkiliyar street. From there they had shouted insults. Meanwhile the woman lay on the ground, as if shattered. When they had looked closely, it had turned out to be Thangam.

Her relatives announced, 'She deserves this and more! She seduced Udayar...shameless bitch...ignoring all of us she found succour in him!'

Hurt by their words, Thangam had pulled herself up and limped back into her hut. But when people from the cheri who were concerned about her went in, the woman had refused to answer them. She had turned on her sisters-in-law with abuse of her own. Her attitude offended even those who felt sorry for her.

'Leave her alone,' they said to each other. 'We'll talk about it tomorrow. Where is she going to go? She needs us.'

Thangam had rejected the sympathy of those who had not said a word to her husband's brothers when they refused to hand over her husband's share of land. She had lived alone, earning her food by toiling every day on Udayar's land. The village women would not talk to her when she went to draw water from the well. No one looked in on her when she fell sick. With pride giving her strength, she had walked the six kilometres from Puliyur to Athur that very night. Wracked by hunger and pain, but most of all by an overwhelming sense of defeat, she had crawled into Kathamuthu's house. But the people of the cheri could not allow themselves such pride. When they could not find Thangam the next morning, the elders ordered a search for her in the village tank and the wells. People looked inside every well and up every tree for her. In the evening, they assembled at the Mariamman temple to decide on a course of action.

It was then that Kathamuthu's messenger, Puttukali, arrived by cycle. Few people knew his real name. His mother had begun calling him Puttukali as a child because of his fondness for ragi balls, and the name had stuck. He did not have any regular job, but was well known in many villages as he carried messages, often news of death. The villagers were eager to hear what news he had brought, and were interested to know that Thangam had gone to Kathamuthu for help. They were somewhat relived to hear that she was in a hospital, under his protection. Puttukali gave a copy of the petition to Pichappillai, a respected elder of the community. He explained to the latter that he should find witnesses who would support the petition, and warned against anybody contradicting the version described in the petition.

'If Kathamuthu says so, we'll do it. He is clever and he must have a plan,' Pichappillai assured Puttukali.

'Let us not create trouble in the village. Kathamuthu will take care of Udayar.' Everyone agreed on that.

~

Valliammai, Thangam's sister-in-law, was inside her house hulling cholam. She had spread the special wild variety that she had fried on a pounding stone. The stone was encircled by a rusted iron ring that she had taken from a broken iron basin at a construction site. A thin layer of the bran from the pounding had settled over Valliammai's torn blue sari and faded blue blouse. It seemed she had forgotten to button her blouse after feeding her child. Each time she lifted the wooden cylinder used to pound the grain, holding it in the middle with one hand and at the shining steel edge with the other, a dark, bulging nipple peeped out. She was careful to control the force she used, in order to avoid pounding the cholam fine. On the top of her head a bunch of short spiky hair stuck out. One could tell that she carried something on her head every day, probably on her way to the field and back home again.

'They beat her up. Good! Why did they leave her alive? That whore thinks too much of herself. She thinks that she's very beautiful. That's why she went after that Udayar. When she loses her shape, he'll throw her out, and she'll be in a state worse than a dog's.'

She voiced her thoughts aloud and nearly powdered the grain instead of just hulling it. She stopped her work when she heard a strange sound. In typical police fashion, the constable hit the old bamboo framing the thatched roof with a lathi.

Shaking the dust off her sari, Valliammai went to the entrance.

'Is this Thangam's house?'

Seeing two policemen, Valliammai pulled up her sari over her blouse. She answered fearfully, 'All of us used to live together in this house. But for the last four years, she has been living alone in that small hut next to the school.'

'What is your relationship with her?'

'I'm her sister-in-law. Our husbands are brothers.'

'What happened to her? Do you know who beat her up? What is the problem?'

'Let me call the menfolk. They are milking the cow.' She rushed to the cattle shed, shouting, 'The police are here, come and answer their questions.' But as she reached the shed she lowered her voice and said, 'There are two of them. You go to the front. I'll call Pichappillai thatha.' She then ran towards Pichappillai's house.

Her husband Manickam, who had been milking the cow, and his brother Sellathurai, who had been cleaning the cattle shed, left their work and hurried to the front of the house. Vasantha, another sister-in-law, had been filling the cattle tub with water. She too rushed to the entrance. Their children, who had been feeding the lambs and playing, also ran to catch up with their parents, shouting excitedly, 'Hai Police! Hai Police!' In just a few minutes, it seemed as if whole cheri had assembled there. Made nervous by the crowd, a number of piglets ran about the street squealing.

With authority, the two policemen shot out their questions. Pichappillai assumed the responsibility of answering them.

'The day before yesterday, at night, Thangam had a stomachache. So she went towards the open toilet ground...'

'Why did she have to go through the upper caste street?'

'What can we do? Earlier, we were using the open ground next to the Parayar school. Now they have built this school...'

'Parayar school?' one of the policemen interrupted.

'That's the panchayat union school, meant for everyone. It has become a Parayar school, filled only with our children. The upper castes don't send their children there, because our children go to that school. They call the school the Parayar school. Even the teachers call it by that name.'

'Enough. We are not here to talk about the school.'

'Anyway, after the school was built, we have been using the open ground beyond the village tank. We go through the Chakkiliyar street and turn north just before the upper caste street.'

'So why did she go near Paranjothi Udayar's house?' countered a policeman.

Voices began to rise in the crowd. Pichappillai pushed away the children who were swarming like bees, 'If anybody makes a noise,

I'll squeeze your beans out. Understand?' Thus warning adults and children alike, he lowered his tone as he turned back to the policemen, 'Udayar's house is on the way, very close to the village tank.'

'And then?'

'Well then, instead of cowering and avoiding the Udayar's wife, she brushed against her. Paranjothi's wife had been sitting outside on a string cot, in her back yard, facing the village tank. She picked a quarrel with Thangam, abusing her by her caste name – Parachi – for walking on the upper caste street. She began to hit Thangam with a broom, and then her brothers and brother-in-law joined her. They were beating her so violently that had we not arrived, Thangam would surely have been murdered.'

'Okay. Who saw the incident?'

A couple of young men got together, 'What do you mean who saw the incident? They had dragged her by her hair to the street and were hitting her with a stout cane! The whole village saw that. How can you ask who saw what had happened?'

'But we need eyewitnesses.'

'In that case please note down Karudayan's son Velu, and Rasu's son Damodran...'

Someone from the crowd shouted, 'If you don't believe us why don't you ask the Chakkiliyars?'

The policemen, followed by all the children from the Parayar street, went to the Chakkiliyar street. As they drew near, the Chakkiliyar children surrounded them.

'People say that Thangam was having an affair with Udayar, and that's why she was beaten up by Udayaramma's relatives. Who knows what the truth is? But we did see those four men hitting her till she bled.'

'No wonder! The rat is out and running naked! How can Udayachi put up with her husband having an affair with a Parachi?' said one policeman to the other.

The other replied, 'It is not as if the Parachi can force the Udayar. If the Udayachi is not smart enough to keep her husband, why should she get others beaten up?'

'Why should it matter to us? Let's finish our enquiries and just write the report.'

'Do you think we should put in writing what the Chakkiliyars had to say?'

'Let's first see what Udayar has to say about the whole thing. The Chakkili beggars may not stand as witnesses if they are dragged to court.'

∾

The entry of the police into the cheri and their subsequent enquiry had genuinely shocked Paranjothi. He had not expected Thangam to act to the extent of filing a police complaint. He had been hopeful of pacifying her by paying her some money. He felt extremely annoyed with his wife and her brothers for causing such trouble.

Had this enquiry been on some other issue, he would have used his power and money and turned the case to his advantage. But, unfortunately, this was about his shameful affair with a Parachi. Besides having ended as a case of criminal assault, his affair had become public knowledge. All the people in the village knew! He cursed Thangam, 'Ungrateful whore! Even if she was hurt, she was hurt by the hand adorned with gold! A Parachi could have never dreamt of being touched by a man like me! My touch was a boon granted for penance performed in her earlier births! And then the dirty bitch betrays me! How can I face the world with my name thus polluted?' He was thoroughly upset. 'My enemies will use my indiscretion to win votes in the next election.'

He did not fear the police, the courts, the expenditure that he might incur, and the nuisance that would follow. Only the caste concerns made him anxious—the exposure of an affair with a

Parachi was humiliating. He would have braved it out even if it had been a murder or a case of criminal assault. But what a disgrace if he had to own up to a relationship with a Parachi! He recalled the beginning of his association with her...

～

Marudhani shrubs formed a thick fence around Udayar's ground-nut field. Thangam was engaged in channelling water from the borewell to the plant beds. She was wearing the flower-printed cotton sari given by the Udayar household for Pongal. Her blouse matched the sari and fitted her well. Below her waist the sari was rolled up to her knees and the upper part lay twisted like a Brahmin's sacred thread, snug between her breasts. Her legs were covered with a thick coat of mud. She was trying to adjust her dishevelled hair with the help of her elbows as her forearms were slick with mud.

Though Thangam was just average looking, her well-arranged, clean teeth and the naive smile that brought forth dimples on her cheeks, attracted Udayar. Thangam appeared attractively different to him. Now that he thought about it, he could only make unfavourable comparisons with Kamalam—her soft flesh and Thangam's muscular body; her round, golden countenance (the effect of turmeric) and Thangam's jutting cheekbones, etc.

Bathing in the tub near the well, he enjoyed watching her secretly. The sun had almost set and there was no one else in the field at that time. She was his servant. Besides, Thangam was no princess or minister's daughter. For that matter, she did not even have a husband. There would not be a soul to rescue her if he imposed himself on her. Moreover, she was only a lower caste labourer.

Therefore, he did not feel restrained in anyway. He looked around. Two labourers, returning home after work were walking at a distance on the grassy bund running through the middle of the field. His brother Perumal was sleeping on a string cot under a tree, quite far from the motor shed. He waited until the labourers walked out of sight and clapped his hands to call Thangam.

Thangam straightened up and looked around as she could not identify the caller. She saw Udayar waving to her. She washed her muddy arms and thought that water must be flowing out of the channel at some point having breeched the mud wall. So she looked around checking for the breach as she walked towards him adjusting her sari.

He hurried her, 'Come quickly.'

As she reached the motor shed, he said, 'Switch off the motor-pump, my hands are wet.'

She hesitated, 'But one part of the field is yet to be watered.'

'That can be done tomorrow. Yesterday Ezhumalai left the hoe in the sugarcane field, go and look for it.'

She switched off the motor-pump and proceeded into the sugarcane field. As she went deeper into the field, Udayar quietly followed her.

She was searching for the hoe in the mud channel running about four feet wide in the middle of the dense sugarcane crop.

'Have you found it?'

Thangam was startled to find him so close.

'Go further.' He drove her to the centre of the field so that no one could see them.

Before she could even guess what Udayar was upto, he grabbed her from behind and held her buttocks tight against his thighs, murmuring harshly, 'Don't shout.' His breath was hot on the skin of her neck and cheeks.

Despite her protests he overpowered her and pushed her down. She resisted him stubbornly. Her resistance only excited him further. Forcefully he subdued her.

Though she had spent her three years of widowhood untouched by a man, she hated succumbing to the loathsome old man's lust. She sobbed with anger sitting in the field.

Thereafter, he made it a routine to have sex with her and slake his lust whenever possible—in the motor shed or in the fields. She no longer resisted him. There was no choice.

Udayar would give her twenty-five or thirty rupees each time. Sometimes he would give her money in the presence of others and order her, 'Get five people from the cheri tomorrow.' And she obliged. She became strict extracting work from those labourers. She always had something or the other to narrate to them about Udayar, his farm or his household matters, though at times she felt disgusted with her life.

One day, it so happened that Kamalam's brother actually saw Udayar and Thangam together. He immediately conveyed the news to his sister. Furious, Kamalam addressed the issue at home by referring to it indirectly. Udayar pretended that he did not understand any of Kamalam's angry insinuations. He assumed that things would settle down in due course. He had hardly expected the sudden turn of events.

The news of policemen entering the cheri reached him at once. He strode into the kitchen and began yelling at Kamalam who was boiling fresh milk.

'Are you happy now? How long have you been scheming to belittle your own husband? You too will surely face the consequences...'

Though Kamalam was nervous, she asked him quietly, without revealing her fear, 'Can't you manage the police?' She apparently had confidence in him.

Realising that it was pointless to argue with her, Udayar stopped at that. By then, an assembly of his caste and community had gathered in his house.

'People say that the police will arrest Perumal and Kamalam's brothers, is that true? Is that woman's condition so serious? We hear that Athur Kathamuthu has taken up her case. Everyone is talking about it.' They had many questions.

Udayar reassured them and sent them away.

FIVE

Whilst the enquiry was going on in Puliyur, a group had gathered in the verandah of Kathamuthu's house. The five people there could easily constitute a panchayat, if numbers alone mattered. Kathamuthu stuck to his limit of hundred millilitres, he never consumed too much arrack. But that was enough to turn him into a loaded gun. Words would pour forth. The Ramayana, the Mahabharata and Gandhi's *My Experiments with Truth* were his granaries, never empty. He could draw freely from them. The poor unlettered labourers and farmers of his caste and acquaintance listened to him with their mouths open. Occasionally, they got up to spit out tobacco.

'Hm...hm...hm...' All Kathamuthu's opinions were rewarded with a chorus of 'hms'. If any one of them dared to express a contrary view, he turned wild, literally demolishing the person. 'What do you know about the government and the way it works? Have you ever entered the collector's office? You have the brains of a sparrow. It's a mystery how your wife sleeps with you! And you have the gall to speak on matters you know nothing about!'

Gowri peeped through the window. She wanted to see the victim who had to swallow these gibes. She could not decide amongst the faces there, so went back to her book.

With the rising moon the jasmine flowers had blossomed. Their heavy fragrance scented the air. Kathamuthu sat with his knees up and his back resting against the wall. Rangasamy hid himself behind the pillar at the edge of the semi-circular steps. The others were sitting on the steps, so that they could stretch their legs if they had to. They had no particular reason for coming together at Kathamuthu's house. They had just fallen in behind Kathamuthu when he had visited the cheri and accompanied him home. When he met a person on his way he would say, 'Why don't you come?' Unable to refuse him, they would have to accompany him, abandoning their own work. But they firmly believed that Kathamuthu would be there when they needed help.

On that day too there were six people, including Rangasamy, who had gathered around Kathamuthu. Though he saw Rangasamy, Kathamuthu refused to acknowledge him.

'Kathamuthu, I heard that the cooperative society is giving loans. Can't you arrange something for us?' an elderly man requested him.

'Yes, of course. That's my main job, isn't it? I have no other work! Do you know when I had breakfast yesterday? At nine in the morning! After that I had to bathe and leave for the police station. I just got half an hour's rest after lunch. Every day something or the other happens and I have to skip breakfast or lunch. My health is spoiled. And I have to work on my land too. You spend all your time in your fields and enjoy the benefit. You have fresh vegetables, fruits. Look at me. I can't pay any attention to agriculture. I have to go every day to the vegetable shop to buy stale, not fresh, food. I have no money to educate my daughter. The rules of the cooperative society are such that without cooking up accounts you can't get a loan—all that takes money. And if I keep doing your work how will I make a living?'

'Kathamuthu, we'll fork out enough to meet some expenses. You please try and get a loan for us.'

'Okay. Now let me have my dinner. You must have finished yours, you people eat by six or seven in the evening.'

'Go ahead, eat your dinner. We are all leaving.' They continued to sit right where they were.

'Kanagavalli, Nagamani, one of you bring me food,' he said raising his voice.

'Wait. The cholam is cooking. It'll take a while,' Kanagavalli replied.

'For the man of the house, they offer gruel!' He spoke to the men, and then shouted back, 'Don't you have any leftover rice from the afternoon? Bring it with some of the mutton curry that you'd made.' The arrack he had consumed begged for food. Chewing on a piece of mutton, he mixed the rice and curry. 'When I was a child, my mother would make porridge and beans. The aroma would waft through the whole village,' he said, swallowing the rice balls one by one.

'You must have had fresh, hot food for your dinner. Look at my plight. Nobody pays any attention to me. They serve me rice left over from lunch. You are all lucky.'

'Kathamuthu, you know our plight. We don't take three meals a day like you do. We definitely don't get rice, we are thankful if we get to eat some kanji!' One of them couldn't help commenting.

Another one offered Kathamuthu betel leaves and areca nut after he had finished eating. Belching with satisfaction, he settled down to narrate his story.

'Yesterday, on this very same verandah, early in the morning, I opened the door to find a dark figure with its head covered—'

'Must have been a mohini pisasu. Arul's wife died recently. Seems she is roaming around as a mohini...'

'Will you stop? I've not even finished the sentence and you start talking about devils and spirits! But I wasn't scared. I asked the creature boldly, "Who the hell are you?" Turned out to be that woman from Puliyur. She's quite tall. Comes up to my chin. She fell at my feet and just refused to get up. Kept moaning "Save me, save me..."' Sekaran set aside his books and went to sit with his father. Gowri could not continue reading any longer. She had to hear the latest interpretation of the story. She crept up to the window and hid herself so that her father could not see her. Hearing Kathamuthu's description of Thangam, both Nagamani and Kanagavalli pricked up their ears.

'A woman of our caste had been the concubine of Paranjothi Udayar. So the men of his house battered her thoroughly.'

'And then?'

'Ayyo…Ayyayyo…' Kanagavalli began wailing and moaning. The people sitting outside heard her and wondered what was going on.

'Will you shut your mouth, or do you need a thrashing?' Kathamuthu raised his voice, but began to laugh.

Nagamani and Kanagavalli giggled like two little girls.

'Then, I got her admitted to the hospital and lodged a complaint at the police station.'

'She had committed adultery and the villagers punished her. What can the police do? They'll just conduct an enquiry and leave it at that,' said one of the visitors doubtfully.

'You fool! Sisterfucker! Is it so simple? Who are the villagers to punish her? If the landowners and upper caste feudal lords take the law into their own hands, why do we need the police? If she is guilty of adultery, what is Udayar guilty of? Who is going to punish him? If your wife is beaten like that, will you talk in the same manner?' Kathamuthu foamed with anger.

'Kathamuthu, forget him. He doesn't know any better.'

'Rangasamy, why are you hiding behind the pillar? Go in and have your food. Upper caste women commit adultery, is that addressed in the panchayat? Can we punish those women? They beat her up because we are lower caste, poor, and have no protection. That's why I have changed the whole story. If this case results in a caste clash, the punishment will be heavy and they can't get our votes. I have not brought Paranjothi Udayar into it because he won't reveal his relationship with a lower caste woman. The number one defendant is Kamalam, his wife. The Udayars will not want to bring their women to court. So they will automatically come to us.'

'Hm…' they chorused.

'Why "hm"? Am I reciting the Ramayanam? You only know how to plough the land and fill your stomachs. Anything more is drum to the deaf. I don't know why I waste my time with you,' said Kathamuthu rising from his seat.

The visitors got up. The oldest among them said, 'What to do? We know you protect our caste people. We are not educated. We have not gone to places like you.'

As they left, Kathamuthu muttered, 'Going places doesn't mean you can become like me. You need talent for that.'

Sekaran had fallen asleep on the floor. Nagamani and Kanagavalli had finished their dinner. They were chewing betel leaves and chatting. Gowri left the window as her father went to his room. Kathamuthu settled down with a thick book, wearing his glasses. It was probably the Mahabharata or the Ramayana. She carried Sekaran inside and came back to the verandah, where the fragrance of the jasmine blossoms soothed her anxious mind. If she were to go to college she would have to stay in a hostel. She could escape from listening to her overbearing father. She slipped into a sweet dream of entering college after her final school examination that year.

A male voice asking for her father interrupted her reverie.

'Is ayya there?'

'Amma, somebody is asking for Appa,' she called out to her mother.

Kanagavalli replied, 'Why don't you tell him yourself?'

'I don't want to call him. If you wish to, you do so,' said Gowri as she lay down next to Sekaran.

Nagamani went to call Kathamuthu, who reappeared on the verandah. He listened to the caller, and then said to Nagamani, 'There's some trouble in the arrack shop between our chaps. They're fighting each other. I'll have to go. It's going to take time, lock the door and go to sleep.'

Pulling on his shirt, Kathamuthu left.

SIX

The police reached Paranjothi's house at about seven in the evening, when the young moon was visible in the sky. Hens in their basket cages were clucking softly. Women who had finished cooking the evening meal sat outside their houses. Some of the children could be heard reading aloud from their books from inside the houses.

Paranjothi invited the policemen to sit on comfortable chairs placed in the central courtyard. After the hours they had spent on their feet in the cheri, the policemen were glad to be able to sit for the first time that evening. The rest of the household stayed inside, the women stopping the children from running out into the courtyard. They gave them sweets to chew, and soon their hands as well as their mouths were sticky. The smell of ghee wafted from the kitchen.

Paranjothi, a prosperous-looking man with a small paunch and skin the colour of wheat, was the epitome of a respectable householder with streaks of thiruneer piously smeared on his forehead. He excused himself and went into the house. When he returned, he was followed by his eldest son, Vadivelu, who brought a plateful of payathamparuppu laddus liberally doused with ghee and two large brass tumblers of hot coffee. At once the atmosphere lightened to cordiality and friendliness. The policemen politely waited until Paranjothi persuaded them to help themselves and then ate the sweetmeats that melted in their mouths. The coffee washed down the snacks and they sat back contented.

Sannasi from the Chakkiliyar street saw the policemen stuffing themselves at Udayar's house and went to report it in the cheri.

A crowd had gathered in front of Udayar's house, curious about the police visit. Vadivelu had to latch the front door shut to prevent them from intruding.

Paranjothi, rather than the policemen, led the enquiry.

'Why don't you begin? Please don't hesitate,' he said.

The policemen handed him a copy of the complaint. Paranjothi read the complaint with trepidation. He then heaved a sigh of relief—the complaint had been framed as caste-related abuse and did not say anything about his relationship with Thangam. He was confident that he could win the police over to his side. As they hesitated to begin, Paranjothi stepped in, decisive and direct in his appeal.

'Look, you'll have to help me get out of this wretched case. You know all the ins and outs. Please guide me.'

'Well, she has been bashed up quite badly. We all wondered how she could have reached Athur in that state,' one of the policemen replied.

'The men were angry and she is arrogant. They shouldn't have done it—but it's over. We ought to be thinking of what to do now, instead of talking about what has been done,' said Paranjothi, single-mindedly steering them back to the issue concerned.

'What can we do? Kathamuthu is extremely clever and he knows many people. He has the cunning of a fox. He should have been born in a lawyer's family! Even the inspector couldn't brush him off. He ordered an immediate enquiry and arrest, in Kathamuthu's presence.' The two policemen looked at each other.

'Money is not a problem,' Paranjothi quickly assured them. 'I'm willing to spend. Please solve this problem for me.'

The policemen excused themselves and moved to a corner of the courtyard, conversing softly. Paranjothi withdrew to have a word with his brother Perumal, who was taking a keen interest in what was happening in the courtyard.

When they assembled again, one of the policemen suggested to Paranjothi, 'Why don't you lodge a counter-complaint?'

'Such as?'

'That she had stolen a transistor and two thousand rupees in cash. Do it as soon as you can. She's in a hospital. You can plant the cash and the transistor inside her house tonight. We'll manage the rest.'

Udayar Paranjothi frowned, feeling hesitant. His discomfort was not because he loved Thangam. Scratching an itch hardly constituted love. But he did feel a twinge of conscience at the thought of foisting such a charge on an innocent Thangam who had had no choice in giving in to him. Perumal who had been listening to everything came to the rescue. 'We have to teach her a lesson, Anna. She can't be allowed to take on an Udayar.'

As Paranjothi remained silent, one of the policemen asked, 'Why are you hesitating? A counter-complaint will only make them withdraw their's. She did not hesitate to bite the hand that fed her, did she? But you refuse to betray her—that's the difference between the upper castes and the lower castes!'

'But do I have to come to the police station?'

'Why don't you send your brother or someone else involved in this case? An FIR has to be registered. If you delay any further it will appear as if you are cooking up a false charge. This is a simple case of theft. If the stolen items are placed in Thangam's house tonight, you can also lodge your complaint tonight, before we make our report tomorrow morning. Don't breath a word about us though,' said one of the policemen.

'We will arrange to leave Puliyur by the last bus to Athur and report at the station at nine tomorrow morning. As he said, do the needful tonight. Otherwise it will be too late,' said the other.

Paranjothi's self-assurance had returned, 'Don't worry about that. We have people who will ensure that it is done.'

As the two policemen rose to leave, Paranjothi disappeared inside a room. They could hear the sound of a safe being opened. He soon returned with two ten-rupee bundles. He handed one bundle to each policeman.

'It's nothing, we are only helping a fellow human being in trouble,' the policemen demurred.

'So am I,' replied Paranjothi thrusting the money into their hands. He also invited them to stay awhile most courteously, 'You are leaving by the last bus, why don't you have dinner here?'

'No, it is already late. We must leave now.'

~

At the arrack shop in Athur town, Kathamuthu's intervention had broken up the fight. Three people had been injured and subsequently despatched to the hospital. The crowd that had gathered began to disperse. The bus coming in from Puliyur slowed down near the arrack shop. The policemen got off and bought themselves half a bottle of brandy. On their way out they saw Kathamuthu. While one of them slipped away, the other was left holding the bottle and cursing his acquaintance with Kathamuthu. Kathamuthu greeted him, 'Are you celebrating something with brandy? I meant to talk to you yesterday after the inspector ordered you to start the enquiries. Are you on your way back from Puliyur?'

'Annachi, I saw him and another policeman getting down from the Puliyur bus,' said Arunachalam, one of Kathamuthu's companions.

'Yes, I am returning from Puliyur,' the policeman said reluctantly.

In a friendly fashion Kathamuthu put his arm around the policeman and patted his bulging pocket. 'Don't tell me it's your payday today?'

The policeman took a step backward, deeply regretting his untimely meeting with Kathamuthu. 'Don't touch me, I don't like that. I am hungry. I have to go home.'

'Don't get so worked up,' said Kathamuthu in a conciliatory tone. 'I just wondered if you had another quarter bottle in your pocket. Anyway, what happened at Puliyur?'

The policeman knew that Kathamuthu had him cornered, what with his finding the bundle of notes. 'Udayar is planning to register a police complaint that Thangam is a thief. Don't ask me more,' he said, slithering away.

Spurred by anger Kathamuthu beckoned Arunachalam, 'Go to Puliyur at once.'

'The last bus for Puliyur left just now.'

'Then hire a cycle and leave.'

'I can't pedal. My foot is swollen, look…' Arunachalam raised his right foot.

Kathamuthu pressed the swollen foot.

'Ayyo, gently please. Should you press so hard?' Arunachalam shrieked.

Wondering what to do, Kathamuthu saw Subramani. Having sat with Thangam in the hospital, he was returning home for his meal. He was walking slowly, his sunken eyes showing his weariness.

'Eley, Subramani!'

On seeing Kathamuthu, Subramani quickened his pace and walked towards him.

'Hire a cycle immediately and rush to Puliyur. Find Pichapillai or Sellamuthu and tell them that I sent you. Ask them to post guards around Thangam's hut for the next few nights.' Subramani stood still, he did not even have the energy to nod in agreement.

'Dey, Arunachalam, if you can't go, can't you at least give Subramani some money to have a glass of tea and hire a cycle?'

Arunachalam replied, 'Where would I have money to spare?' But Kathamuthu had grabbed the ten-rupee note from Arunachalam's shirt pocket.

'Oh no, those ten rupees are for hiring labour to plough my field tomorrow.'

'Who wants your money? Come to my house tomorrow and I'll return it,' said Kathamuthu walking away. Arunachalam mentally wrote off his ten rupees. It was his misfortune to have met Kathamuthu that night.

SEVEN

It was nearly midnight by the time Subramani reached Puliyur. He considered sleeping in the Mariamman temple and waking Pichapillai early in the morning. But he decided against it and rang the bicycle bell in front of Pichappillai's house. No one answered.

Subramani called out, 'Thatha, thatha.'

'What is it? Who is it, at this hour?' Pichappillai, aroused from deep sleep, emerged unwillingly.

'Thatha, it's Subramani from Athur.'

Pichappillai took him to the street lamp to study his face.

'What's the matter?'

Subramani lowered his voice and repeated Kathamuthu's instructions. 'The Udayars are going to plant some money in Thangam's hut tonight. They have lodged a false complaint against her. So Kathamuthu ayya sent me to warn you. He requested you to post a couple of men to guard Thangam's hut.'

'What a damn nuisance. Whom can I call at this hour? Let that woman go to hell. Kathamuthu need not have taken up her cause with such enthusiasm,' Pichappillai grumbled. 'Well, now that I'm up...Subramani, go and get Kathan, Chinnasamy and Rasendran from the Mariamman temple. The youngsters usually sleep there. Wake them up. I'll get my betel leaves and follow you.'

Before long, Subramani had five young men moved to Thangam's house. Pichappillai provided two old bamboo cots for them to use. They sat on the cots, smoking their beedis. Pichapillai himself sat in a corner of the school verandah amongst the goats tethered there for the night, chewing his betel leaves.

Just as the first rooster began to crow, Pichappillai saw two shrouded figures approaching the school. He shouted, alerting the boys.

The lads jumped down at once and went running towards the figures. The two figures sped away, vanishing into the upper caste street.

EIGHT

Arumuga Padayachi and Saminatha Padayachi hurtled into Paranjothi Udayar's cow shed, latched the tin door shut and gasped in relief.

'Did it go well?'

The question came from Perumal Udayar and Kamalam's brothers. They were sitting on a string cot, and in the dim light from the hurricane lamp looked like conspirators.

'No,' said the two panting.

'What do you mean, no? Arumugam, what happened?'

'Sami, didn't you see us come in running for our lives?' Saminathan replied as Arumugam stood heaving for breath.

'There were four or five men with stout sticks. And somebody shouted a warning...we couldn't let ourselves be caught, that's why we ran away.'

The four men were gripped by fear. If the evidence had not yet been planted, it meant that the complaint they had filed against Thangam was invalid. It meant that arrest warrants would soon be issued for these miscreants.

Having heard the Padayachi men come running, Paranjothi Udayar, who had been unable to sleep, came out to the cow shed.

Kamalam followed him to ask fearfully, 'Wasn't it possible?'

Paranjothi turned to her and said, 'Go back to sleep.'

'What are you going to do now?'

'We need to discuss that.'

It was dawn and a chill morning wind was blowing. Paranjothi was jolted by the electric lamp turned on in his neighbour

Ramalinga Reddiar's cow shed. He urged his men to put out their lamp, keen to keep his villainy secret.

Ramalinga Reddiar's servant, Kaliyan, untied the cows and brought them to the cattle trough. Their noisy slurping could be heard next door. They also heard the back door of Reddiar's house open. Reddiar's wife Santha came out of the still dark house into the shed, her eyes dazzled by the sudden light.

If one could climb on a string cot and stand on one's toes, Ramalinga Reddiar's back yard, cow shed and dry latrine could be seen from Paranjothi Udayar's house. And Paranjothi made the effort to peer over the wall into Reddiar's house.

Santha turned off the light in the cow shed and glanced around. After she ascertained that no one was watching, she walked towards Kaliyan who now was tying up the cows.

Kaliyan had been slaving for Reddiar's household for many years. He was an extremely skilled worker. His haystacks were built so well that even a storm could not blow them apart. If he wove thatch not a drop of rain would leak through the roof. If he dug the water channels in the rice field, they would be as strong as stone-built dams. If he harvested a field, not a stalk of grain would be wasted. He was also equally skilled in pleasuring Santha. Santha's lust could have also been inspired by his beauty and youth.

Mornings were convenient for her. Ramalinga Reddiar drank heavily and settled down to sleep only late in the night, therefore he would be snoring at dawn. Her children would not stir until she woke them up with coffee. While her mother-in-law was bedridden, her father-in-law was usually up at the crack of dawn. But he would remain seated on the front verandah chewing betel leaves. He would prove his usefulness by harassing Kaliyan when he passed through the front of the house, leading the cows to pasture. 'Dey, watch out...' 'Where is the cow's bell?' 'Have you fed them water?' 'That cow's stomach seems distended...' 'You need to shave their horns.' 'Don't be arrogant.' 'Do you massage oil on your body?'

The irritated Kaliyan would make a short and appropriate reply, and move away muttering, 'Old fool!'

When Paranjothi Udayar looked over the wall, he found Kaliyan in the tight embrace of Santha. In absolute silence Kaliyan roughly pushed her on top of the hay spread for feeding the cows.

'Disgusting,' spat out Paranjothi as he stepped down.

'What is it?' enquired Kamalam anxiously. The rest were eager to know what he had seen.

He turned on the light in their shed, saying, 'How can I describe what I saw?'

'Let them grab at what they can,' he murmured to himself.

As soon as the light flooded her back yard, Santha shoved Kaliyan aside and began yelling at him, 'Lazy fool, you were supposed to go to the cheri and hire labour for sowing, not snooze on the hay spread for the cattle.' Her severity towards him during the day would be in proportion to her desire for him during the early morning hours.

In fact, sometimes her harshness to Kaliyan would spur Ramalinga Reddiar to intervene, 'Why do you scold him so much?'

Something about Santha's abuse of Kaliyan inspired Paranjothi to decide on a specific course of action. 'Where are you going?' asked Kamalam.

'Do you have any sense? Asking me where I'm going when I'm on my way…'

He covered his naked torso with a stretch of white cotton and retied his veshti. He beckoned to Saminatha Padayaci and Arumuga Padayachi and swiftly walked out of the house. His brother and brothers-in-law followed him out wondering what his plan was. Paranjothi halted at the street corner.

'You went to the cheri to hire labour for sowing with no intent to harm anyone. But you were attacked and chased out for no reason at all. Is that clear?'

They had walked up to Ramalinga Reddiar's house. The old man peered at them and called out to Kaliyan. Santha came running.

'Udayar...' Santha said aloud for the old man's benefit.

'Kaliya, open the gate. Why are they here at such an odd time? Santha, wake up my son.'

Within a short period of time it looked as if the whole street had gathered in front of Ramalinga Reddiar's house. Udayar, Reddiar, Mudaliar, Padayachi—all the upper castes had convened, unkempt and unwashed.

'Did you know that men who had gone to the cheri to hire workers were beaten up?'

'Padayachis attacked by Parayars?'

'Were they only blows? Was someone knifed?'

'Why attack someone who went to hire workers?'

'Who knows? Didn't the police visit the cheri yesterday?'

'Will this happen anywhere else?'

'Send someone to the neighbouring village quickly. The seedlings can't be left unplanted. Maybe we should hire labour from the Chakkiliar street. The planting might not be good enough, but we'll have to make do.'

The inhabitants of the upper caste street expressed different opinions and dispersed. But the community leaders remained seated in Ramalinga Reddiar's house. Santha served them coffee in small brass tumblers.

'Paranjothi, I heard that the police came to your house yesterday?' enquired Ramalinga Reddiar.

'The Paraya bitch who was working for me had misbehaved, so my men punished her. She went to Athur and took Kathamuthu's help to register a police complaint.'

'You should have hacked her to pieces and buried her!'

'Let that be. How do we deal with today's incident? We need workers to plant the seedlings.'

'All the farmland in this village has been ploughed and made ready for planting. Let's pay some more and hire workers from neighbouring villages. We can also hire the Chakkiliyars. The Chakkiliyars and Parayars here have been hostile towards each other for the past three years. So let's call them.'

'But for how long…?'

'If the Parayars starve for a few days they will come of their own accord.'

'What if Kathamuthu interferes?'

'If they don't give in before that, we will burn the cheri to the ground. If the Parayars cannot serve the upper castes they might as well die,' said Ramalinga Reddiar, the flabby flesh on his chest jiggling.

'Don't say that aloud,' cautioned Paranjothi.

'I am not afraid.' Reddiar pointed to his crotch, 'I can't be shaken.' Fuelled by caste pride, none of them found the gesture obscene.

'Will you stand by that?'

'Udayar, just do what you have to do. Don't hesitate.' Ramalinga Reddiar then called out, 'Santha!' and his wife came out to respectfully bid them farewell.

It was not as if the upper castes were incapable of comprehending the true nature of the events that had taken place. But the Parayars had attempted to beat the Padayachis (with stout sticks!)—that simply could not be allowed. They had to be taught a lesson.

NINE

As the sun rose, people heading for the open toilet beyond the tank were surprised to see the young men occupying narrow cots in front of Thangam's hut. Valliammai, carrying a load of cow dung on her head, noticed the stout sticks and long knives underneath the cots. She stopped to question them.

'Eley, Ramachandra, why are you sleeping here?'

Half asleep, he looked up and told her, 'It is to save your very dear sister.'

'Boys, be careful! Don't get into a quarrel with the Udayars on account of that worthless bitch. They're dangerous. They won't hesitate to burn down the entire cheri.'

'Those days are gone, when they burned people alive! They can't even pull out our pubic hair,' shouted Rasendran.

'Ey, she is your cousin. Watch your words,' Chinnasamy cautioned him.

'First they beat her and then they want to brand her a thief! Now they'll burn us alive? Didn't he enjoy sleeping with her in every nook and corner of his field? Didn't he enjoy the fruits of her labour? How can we put up with this any longer? I'd like to chop all those shits into small pieces.'

The five young men stayed there the whole day, slumped on the string cots, guarding Thangam's house. No one from the upper caste street came to hire people for work in their fields.

Only the Chakkiliyar women set out, their hair oiled and neatly combed. The Parayar women of the cheri had not been called. The previous day, both groups of women had together removed the rice shoots from the seed bed, bundled them and placed them in the ploughed fields, in readiness for planting them the next day. The Parayar women, who were usually called for such work, had risen early and cooked food for the morning and afternoon. They had expected to be called to plant the seedlings.

Disappointed and annoyed at the sight of Chakkili women proceeding to work, they complained to the old man Pichappillai, who was sitting in the Mariamman temple, as though they were appealing to the goddess herself.

'This is atrocious, Mama! Yesterday they told us to be ready for work and today they ignore us!'

'Thatha, why are you keeping quiet? We pulled out those seedlings yesterday and these women are going to pull out their hairs?!'

'Look Chittappa, it seems they are hiring workers from other villages for six and seven rupees instead of three. If they can pay double the amount for people from neighbouring villages, why couldn't they have paid us a rupee or fifty paise more?'

The place was in an uproar with the women noisily complaining to Pichapillai.

Rasendran, Chellappandi, Chandran and other young men joined in with a different set of protestations.

'They have rejected our work, we should never work for them again. We should rather die than work for them. In case they come to us again we ought to ask for the same wage they are now paying to workers from Arumadal and Kilappuliyur.'

The women chorused their support.

'Only if we demand more wages, will they think twice before refusing us work.'

'They may own land for miles at a stretch. But the sight of it can be beautiful only when humans toil on it. Can paddy be reaped with the help of magic? They have such plentiful harvests that only elephants and horses can separate the paddy on the threshing floor. They have stored all of it and prospered by selling it for years together…If we ask for a fifty-paise increase in our wages, they feel that their life will come to an end!' lamented an old lady.

Pichappillai waited for the anger to simmer down. Then he said, 'Why waste your time grumbling? Go back to your homes, have your breakfast in leisure and take a nap as well. Those bastards cannot go anywhere. Soon we'll have the Mariamman festival. I'll talk to Kathamuthu, we'll see.'

Pichapillai thus managed to pacify the crowd of women milling around him. But these developments in Puliyur worried him. Only the bonded labourers went to work in the upper caste households that day. Men too were prevented from going to work on their own.

Women who usually bathed their children once a week attended to their newborn babies and toddlers with warm water. A lucky few who owned small holdings of dry land near the rocky hills, cultivated cholam, kambu and other grains for six months of the year. They busied themselves preparing seeds for the next season. They mixed water and red soil, coated the yellow seeds with the mixture, and laid them out to dry in the sun. That day, some women set to work repairing the mud walls of their houses with a paste made of clay and cow dung. No one could stay idle.

The men worked on different jobs. They dug out and deepened the manure pit where cow dung and dirt had collected. Where there were gaps in the hedge, they filled them with dry thorn shrubs. Some men made ropes from plant fibre. Others strengthened their haystacks. Some stacked firewood.

There was only a month left until the Mariamman festival. There would be goat meat from the sacrifice and fresh sticky rice, accompanied by the musical rustling of new clothes, and new turmeric and ceremonial raw rice. The entire cheri of Puliyur would be in a joyous mood. There would be sweet pongal, ragi gruel, sour pork curry, chilli pork and homemade arrack to eat and drink. After a few deep swigs of the locally brewed liquor, pulling the chariot of the goddess would be fun. Every year the men eagerly looked forward to the festival day.

Sitting atop a chariot, Mariamman in her red cotton sari with its bright zari border would visit each household. Everyone in the family, along with their relatives from neighbouring villages, would offer coconuts, bananas and five or ten rupees. The priest would break each coconut and return an exact half to the family. Before the deity reentered the temple, someone appointed to represent the upper castes would pay their respect in a similar fashion. Having received the upper castes' respect, the deity would be satisfied and return to her sanctum.

Pamphlets asking for donations had already been printed. The deposit for the loud speaker had been paid. A new red sari had been purchased for the deity. The veshti and payment for the Valluva Pandaram were ready.

But the atmosphere was tense. The smooth conduct of the festival appeared doubtful. As a first step, the upper castes had kept the cheri people out of work. And the young men from the cheri were ready for violence. Moreover, the cheri inhabitants had begun to dream of increased wages.

TEN

That morning, rumours of upper caste men having been chased out the cheri when they had gone to engage workers rapidly spread through the village. The villagers also came to know that the men who had been chased were Arumuga Padayachi and Saminatha Padayachi, who owned small farms but spent most of their time working on Paranjothi Udayar's vast farm. That Parayars could attack Padayachis astonished and angered them, they weren't inclined to question the facts. Truth had gone into hiding. Even though both communities were poor and had similar lifestyles, the Padayachis who were slightly higher up the social ladder, took offence. They were more concerned with testing their own strength. Even those not directly affected ranged themselves with the rest of the village against the people of the cheri.

Small farmers who desperately needed labourers to finish planting the seedlings had to heed the village restrictions. Their anger, however, was conveniently directed towards the Parayars. They had to make do with each other's help, driven by the fear of exceeding the short period within which the planting had to be done.

Udayar and other wealthy upper caste men tried to entice workers from surrounding villages. But Arumadal, Sirumadal, Melapuliyur, Kilapuliyur, etc. were also in need of similar seasonal agricultural work. Moreover, Kathamuthu had strong support in the cheris in those villages. Their attempts to offer double the wages did not completely succeed.

But Udayar and his cohorts were satisfied that they had stirred and fanned caste prejudices and hostilities. They rested in the certainty that a caste clash was imminent and could not be prevented.

~

Kamalam's casteism had exceeded all limits. A twelve-year-old boy from the cheri worked as a bonded labourer in her house. His task was to attend to the cattle. He was required to bring hay from the haystack, collect green fodder and grind punnakku to feed the cattle. As payment, he was given one hundred kilograms of paddy a year. Waste and spoiled food was normally dumped on him. The boy ate what he was given down to the last grain. He was hare-lipped, with hair like a bird's nest. Flinging threats and abuses at him was part of Kamalam's daily routine. That morning when he had finished his chores and sneaked through the back door to wait for his food, Kamalam sneered at him. She even reduced his due of leftover food by throwing the remains into the cattle trough. Then she contemptuously waved a broom at him, 'Grind the cotton seeds well, or I'll grind yours!' He thought she was joking and smiled, hiding his hare-lip with his palm. But even he was forced to wonder at the 'Paraya! Paraya!' that studded her talk.

~

The Padayachi widow Mangalavati (called Nondichi by the villagers) had a good-looking daughter, Lalitha. Every day Lalitha went by bus from Puliyur to Athur, to learn tailoring. Elangovan from Puliyur cheri also travelled by the same bus to Athur, where he worked as a peon in a bank. Travelling together had helped create an intimacy between them. They continued to take the morning bus to Athur even as tension built up in Puliyur.

'Elango, don't be offended, but why are your people so violent? I believe they nearly attacked those who came to hire labourers, is that true?' asked Lalitha, emphasising 'your people'.

'You sound very concerned today, but when your people assaulted Thangam, why didn't you raise any questions then?' Elango too emphasised 'your people'.

'Are you talking in support of that whore?'

'If she is a whore, what is your Udayar?'

'He is a man! He can do anything that pleases him.'

'So if I wink at another woman, will that be okay with you?'

'Don't try to be smart. You are showing your true colours, aren't you?'

Hurt by her words, Elango shouted, 'What is wrong with me? What do you mean?' Most of the passengers in the bus turned to look at them. Lalitha burned with humiliation. People already gossiped about her affair with a lower caste man. And he had yelled at her in front of everyone, as though she were his wife.

She blurted out 'You've proved your caste, haven't you?'

Elangovan felt as though somebody had knocked him out. He took great pains to hide his caste identity. He wore good clothes. He had changed his language considerably, and behaviour as well. Her words fell like blows on his heart. He wanted to beat her senseless. But he felt completely paralysed and speechless. He stopped the bus and got down.

Though she knew that her words had caused him pain, Lalitha justified herself, 'How dare he mention winking at another woman to me?' The bus continued on its way to Athur.

ELEVEN

The protection for Thangam's hut continued into the third day. For two days, the people of the cheri had gone without work.

Pichappillai had gone to Athur to talk things over with Kathamuthu. But Kathamuthu had left Athur to attend the funeral of some village head. Pichappillai waited till late in the night for his return. Kathamuthu expressed deep concern about Puliyur. He promised to report the situation to the police and the taluk administration, and visit Puliyur himself in a couple of days.

∿

Kannamma, an old woman who lived in one corner of the Puliyur cheri, was known as 'crazy Kannamma'. Though she was strong for her age, her eyesight was poor. She would take the cholam out and leave the measure in the gunny bag, and then accuse the neighbours of stealing it. 'May they die of plague!' she would curse and wail. People who visited her would stretch out their empty palms before leaving to let her know that they weren't pilfering anything from her house. But if she misplaced a small item – for example, the extra-long needle for stitching gunny bags, the funnel for pouring kerosene into lamps every evening, the iron fire-tongs or the lids of bottles – she would immediately suspect the most recent visitor. She would then go to the Mariamman temple and pray to the goddess to punish those who had visited her house. 'Bring them down with paralysis and diarrhoea and anything else you can for the rest of their lives,' she would beseech the deity.

Two years ago, her daughter-in-law had committed suicide, leaving behind two children, aged four and two. The daughter-in-law had become depressed when her husband, who was usually good to her, had got drunk on toddy and called her a whore. So she had hanged herself to death. Though Kannamma urged her son to marry again, he resisted, continuing to grieve for his wife. Therefore, Kannamma had to do all the household work and look after the children as well.

To see her groping about, struggling to manage her household chores would make one feel sympathetic, till she unleashed her tongue—she could be really vicious. Hence, she was considered an object of ridicule in the cheri. Late in the evening, Kannamma began to cook for the night. She sifted the flour short-sightedly, trying to separate the broken grains of cholam. She intended to add the broken grains to boiling water, cook them partially and then add the flour gradually to prevent the formation of lumps. The mixture had to be stirred with two ladles. When it was nearly done, the burning pieces of wood would be removed from the fire and the gruel left to simmer on the remaining heat. Finally, the thick gruel would be scooped into a mud pot, patted into balls and dropped into water.

Kannamma mixed the flour and looked for water. There wasn't a drop left. Her son had not yet come home after driving the cattle to their shelter. The children who had been crying in hunger had fallen asleep. She tried to wake them, but they stubbornly remained asleep. She finally bent down and muttered 'peanut candy' in their ears.

That made them jump and sit up straight.

'Where?' they demanded, looking around for the candy.

'Come, we'll go to the shop and buy them.' The disappointed children followed her, irritable and weepy.

Kannamma peered at the cooking fire. She decided it was too strong and pulled out one of the burning stems.

'There's no water, not even to wet a parched throat,' she muttered, picking up the brass water pot. She did not want her son to come back home tired and thirsty after a long day, and find no water.

She took the children to the tumbledown, dusty shacks that were the local shops. On the way she noticed a man dressed in a white veshti and shirt, standing at a distance and staring. 'Let him be broken and tossed into the funeral pyre.' She clasped the fingers of both her hands together and cracked her knuckles, cursing him.

Kannamma called out, 'Anyone there?' when she reached the shop. Amongst the grocery items on a shelf were stale peanut candies, sesame balls, fried beaten rice and white puffed rice, all in glass jars with rusted lids. An old woman shuffled forward.

Villagers called her Mottachi because of the thin, wispy hair that barely covered her scalp. She looked at Kannamma with mistrust.

'What do you want?'

'Two peanut balls.'

'Do you have money?'

'Who will come to your shop without money?'

'Okay. Take these and give me the money.'

Kannamma gave the children one peanut ball each. She reached for the inner edge of her sari, where she usually tied her coin purse made of cloth. She couldn't find it. She had to literally remove the sari in her attempt to find the purse, and she was wearing neither skirt nor blouse.

'What are you trying to show?' exclaimed the shopkeeper, waiting for her twenty paise.

'Wait. I am searching.'

'How long should I wait? It's always like this with you.'

'I think I must have left my purse near the tank when I washed myself there this afternoon.'

'I don't know about that and I can't accept any excuses. Get the money and come back quickly.'

Relieved to get away, Kannamma stepped out of the shop.

'That horrible Mottachi will die the worst death possible. Even this scrap of a shop will be lost, and she will have to beg for food one day,' she mumbled as she hobbled to the well.

A crowd of women stood around the well, waiting for their turn to draw water.

'Oh, dear children. I am blind. I can't draw water. Please somebody fill my pot. These children are hungry and thirsty.'

No one offered to help. One woman said, 'You have just come. We have all been waiting. I've left my young one at home. You don't have children crying for milk. Wait your turn.'

Kannamma waited. Another woman spoke to her, 'Why don't you stand a little away from me? Can't you see that I'm standing at the edge of the well? Don't push me in.'

Finally one of them took pity on her. 'Paati, let me fill mine first, then I'll help you with yours.'

'You have four pots to fill. I have only one. Please fill mine first,' Kannamma pleaded.

'This is exactly what I don't like about you. You will grind chillis on my head if I let you.'

'No...no...I'll wait.'

As the woman drew water and filled her four big pots, she spoke of Kannamma's daughter-in-law. 'Your grandchildren are pretty as a pair of parakeets. How could their mother choose to orphan them?'

The remark brought tears to Kannamma's dim eyes.

The woman gave her sister the pots she had filled and began filling the rest. Kannamma did not notice that, absorbed as she was in her sorrow.

Flames, meanwhile, leaped to the roof of her hut.

TWELVE

The fire raced outwards from Kannamma's hut, greedy to devour the rest of the neighbourhood. People who were eating ran out of their homes, abandoning their food. Everyone who could, snatched up containers, whether of aluminium or clay, and rushed to the public well. Some Chakkiliyar huts burned too. Pichamuthu Padayachi's roof caught fire and the Mangalore tiles exploded. Had the wind blown in any other direction, the cheri would have gone up in flames.

Everyone pitched in to fight the fire—men, women and children of the cheri and the Chakkiliyar community. Three huts in the cheri were completely destroyed, while two were partially damaged. One Chakkiliyar hut was burned to the ground and one was partially damaged. About thirty tiles of Pichamuthu Padayachi's roof had been shattered by the fire.

Kannamma, whose house had been reduced to ashes, rolled on the street and wept that the thatch had been woven just three months ago. She swore, invoking the names of various deities, that she had doused the cooking fire before going out.

Gradually she began to curse, 'Paavi, you set fire to my house! Will your funeral pyre burn? Hanging around and watching my house! Was it to set fire to it? I would have thrown you into my cooking fire if I had guessed!' She repeatedly screamed accusations at that unknown man.

The residents of the cheri and the Chakkiliyar street began to question her excitedly, 'Who is he? What did he look like?'

'Sami, How would I know? I am half blind. I could only make out that he was wearing a white veshti and a shirt.' The hungry children sobbed along with their grandmother.

'From her description he sounds like an upper caste man,' said someone in the crowd. The rest joined in support of the theory as though they had been waiting to hear a mention of it. 'Because we didn't go for planting work they decided to burn our houses.'

That Kannammma was unreliable, had poor eyesight and rarely hesitated to blame innocent people were forgotten as emotions rode high amongst both the young and the old.

Valliammai reminded Rasendran, 'Rasendra, don't you remember, I warned you that they would burn the cheri down? Haven't my words proved true?'

Rasendran had heard of many incidents of people of untouchable castes being burned alive, but he had firmly believed that it would never happen in his village. He and many others had concluded with certainty that the upper castes had started the fire.

Ponnusamy from the Chakkiliyar street interjected, 'Okay, they set fire to Parayar houses because you chased their men away and stopped going to work. But what did we do? Why were our houses also burned down?'

'You thought, "Let the Parayars deal with their fate," and went to work for Udayar, now you can see how you've been paid for that. For us, Parayan, Pallan, Chakkiliyan, Valluvan and Vannan may be different. For them, we are all the same—all untouchables. Do you think they would make *us* stand outside their houses and take *you* inside and feed you milk and rice? As long as we continue to differentiate among ourselves and beg for their favour, they will continue to manoeuvre and hammer us into submission.'

An elder of the community, Sellamuthu spoke up, 'We have suffered enough. Let each man grab a torch or a sickle, let us test our strength!'

The young men, eager to plunge into a real fight, jumped at this. So far Pichappillai had listened and said nothing. The others were waiting for him to speak. But an unnatural silence descended when they saw the headlights of a vehicle approaching. When they saw that it was a police jeep, they began to get excited again. The women and children were instructed to go back into their houses.

'We are right! It's been half an hour since the fire, even the fire engine hasn't arrived. Those upper caste villains set the fire, then fearing for their own necks, called the police.'

The crowd milled around in anger, as the policemen stepped out of their jeep. Another jeep followed carrying the tahsildar.

'Look at that! The tahsildar! Even for sanctioning leave for his staff, he'll not sign a form unless a five-rupee note is clipped with it. The gutter-rat! Why does he come here?'

'One of our women was beaten like a dog and no one showed up that time. We reported to the tahsildar that the upper caste landowners had stopped our work. No one showed up then too. Now our houses have been burned and as we take up our weapons these rats are here.' The educated and the unlettered grumbled.

It was ten o'clock in the night. The last bus from Athur brought a messenger from Kathamuthu. He found Pichapillai in the crowd and whispered in his ear that Kathamuthu was on his way, and that no one should say anything to the police till he arrived.

The moment the cheri caught fire, the rich Reddiars, Ramalingam and Arunachalam, had joined forces with Paranjothi Udayar. In that village, the Reddiars and Udayars were equal in number and status. They maintained difference of opinion with regard to village and political affairs, but joined hands over labour and wage issues. These two dominant communities owed political allegiance to the ruling party, so the new rules of land reform could hardly be implemented. Both communities had filed a combined affidavit when a case was registered against benami holdings. The Padayachis were also very strict in observing caste rules. Unlike the Reddiars and the Udayars, however, they did not depend on hired labour as their land holdings were much smaller. Even the farmers' movement of the last few years could not break down the barriers of caste and unite the small farmers of the backward Padayachi community with the lower caste community.

Even amongst the lower castes, hierarchies existed—Pallars were agricultural labourers, Parayars were drummers and menials, and the Chakkiliyars were cobblers. The first grade – the Pallars – were absent in Puliyur. The Pallars considered themselves superior to the rest. The Parayars considered themselves higher than the Chakkiliyars, who in turn considered themselves superior to the Para-vannars, the washer community. The Para-vannar men washed clothes for the lower castes and the women worked as midwives for them. Similar to almost all other human communities, the women were considered to be lower than the men. Everyone established their worth by pointing to those beneath them.

News arrived that the sub-collector of Athur was coming. Meanwhile the tahsildar and the inspector went around the village, assessing the extent of damage. They made estimates of the value of properties lost in the fire and noted owners' names. They also recorded Kannamma's testimony.

A petromax lamp was brought to the large tamarind tree located between the village and the cheri. Some string cots and benches were carried out from the upper caste houses. Chairs were brought from Paranjothi's house. The rich upper caste men sat on the benches on one side. Lower caste men and women stood about forty feet away from. them. Pichapillai, Sellamuthu and a few other cheri elders sat on the roots of the tamarind tree. The tahsildar and the inspector sat on the chairs. When they signalled the lower caste men to come closer, the latter answered that they were waiting for Kathamuthu.

'We are here because their houses caught fire. We are here to ensure shelter and food for those who lost their homes. Why are they so unresponsive? Why can't they cooperate a little? If we were to speak only to Kathamuthu, we could have done that at Athur. Why should we have come here? We came here to help them and they are not the least bit grateful,' the tahsildar and the inspector grumbled in irritation. The children who were still awake were flocking around the petromax lamp. The tahsildar's men chased them away. The cheri crowd's cynical stares and untidy looks further annoyed the inspector and the tahsildar.

At last Kathamuthu arrived, seated on a bicycle, pedalled by someone else. He jumped off and folded his hands in greeting to the tahsildar and the inspector first, and then the Reddiars and Udayar. 'Sami! At last you have come. Please see my house. It is nothing but ashes.' Kannamma beat her chest hard with both hands and stumbled forward to fall at Kathamuthu's feet. Her son hurried to support her. She was a pathetic figure, lamenting at such a high pitch that all the cheri women joined in, beating their chests and keening. Kathamuthu stood quietly while they vented their grief. Kannamma refused to get up, so he had to lift her up against her will with the help of her son. He too felt moved by her grief.

The crowd conducted Kathamuthu to the burned huts. He viewed them silently. Then he asked Pichappillai and Sellamuthu, 'How did this happen?'

'Kannamma says someone set fire to her hut. But no one saw anything.'

'But whoever set the fire couldn't do it in the presence of witnesses, right?' Kathamuthu quipped.

The cheri youth surrounded Kathamuthu and pestered him, 'Sir, give us permission, and we'll deal with those bastards. We'll return with their intestines as our garlands!'

'Eley, your mothers feed you and you not do any work. It is the surplus fat that makes you speak like that. While you return with their intestines as garlands, will they be plucking flowers? Those monsters will swallow you and the entire village.'

'The Chakkiliyars are on our side,' assured Rasendran.

'If you and the Chakkiliyars don't work in their fields, they will hire Padayachis. Will you all starve?'

'We starve and die anyway,' said an old man in the crowd.

'Let us die fighting them, instead of living such shameful lives.'

'Don't talk like that! You're being wild and hot-headed,' Kathamuthu berated them. 'That's not the way. Why don't you suggest something practical? If you die, please understand, that's your loss. It costs the upper castes nothing.'

Kathamuthu wanted to prevent the spark of violence from getting out of control. He wondered as to how to transform the situation and gain something productive from it. 'What is practical? We will bargain for better compensation for our losses. We'll demand to go to work from tomorrow. Let us make sure they pay us better wages. We should make it expensive for them to crush us another time. Remember, we have to live in this village. The village and cheri have to coexist. We can't live as enemies and in fear.'

Kathamuthu argued persuasively. After the cheri people's demands were specified and listed clearly, Kathamuthu swiftly walked towards the tamarind tree.

THIRTEEN

The tahsildar and the inspector sat at the head of the gathering, Paranjothi Udayar and other upper caste men on their right and Kathamuthu on their left. Pichappillai and Sellamuthu were about to seat themselves again on the protruding tamarind roots, but Kathamuthu stopped them and told them to sit on a cot. One was vacated for them and they sat on it hesitantly. The tahsildar sought the inspector's approval to open the meeting.

'News reached us at Athur that there was a problem of law and order in Puliyur. We heard that it was a caste clash between the Kudiyanavars and the Harijans, and that some houses were burned down. The inspector of police and I are here to make enquiries and do the needful. We shall be fair to both sides. I suggest that one person represent each party. When the representatives speak no one should interrupt and there should not be any abusive language. Please maintain silence while we listen to them. This is for your own good.'

The inspector called his subordinates and instructed them to check the crowd for weapons. They moved through the throng. One officer kept an eye on the young men, who were still huddled together, slightly apart from the crowd.

Kathamuthu began first, 'Tahsildar sir, as we are the injured party please allow me to speak first.'

The tahsildar looked at Paranjothi Udayar who indicated his consent with a nod of his head. His smile, and the smiles on his cronies' faces, implied that it did not matter to them if Kathamuthu spoke first. The people of the cheri gave their full attention to Kathamuthu.

'As far as I can remember, the upper castes and the Harijans of this village have always lived in harmony. They have been like fathers and sons of the same family. Certainly there have been times when they have had differences of opinion, but those died down quickly. Am I right? Pichappillai, you are an elder of this village. You know how it has always been. Right?'

Both Pichappillai and Sellamuthu swayed their heads in agreement.

'I am married to a woman from this village. My wife's elder brother is sitting here beside me. I am related in some way to most of the people here. After I became president of the panchayat union, I arranged to have a well for drinking water dug in the cheri. The school here was established through my efforts. I had the street lights installed. I am still trying to get an electric connection for the well, so that drinking water can be supplied through pipes. Though I am no longer in power, even today the people of this cheri respect me. I continue to be a part of the happenings, good or bad. Isn't that so, Sellamuthu?'

'Yes, yes.'

'I still remember,' Kathamuthu continued, 'that I was the first one to wear sandals and walk on the upper caste street. In those days, our men had to get off their bicycles as soon as they entered that street and walk the length pushing the vehicle. But I had my hair cut, unlike others, and cycled on their streets. They couldn't swallow that, but had to put up with it because I was politically active.'

The tahsildar and police inspector looked impatiently at their watches.

'Why am I saying these things now? To illustrate that circumstances are better now. Those days are gone. Our children are attending school. The lucky ones get government jobs. A few men have started their own businesses. But even in these changed times, atrocities occur in villages like Puliyur.'

He paused and continued, 'A few days ago, a woman was whipped by upper caste men in this village. They set fire to the cheri—'

Ramalinga Reddiar and Arunachala Reddiar protested, 'We will swear in any temple, we are not responsible for the fire.'

Kathamuthu, disgruntled at the interruption, said, 'Tahsildar sir, I have not finished yet.'

The tahsildar looked at Paranjothi Udayar, who in turn silenced the Reddiars with a glare.

'I am coming to the point. In Athur as well as the surrounding villages, a labourer gets five to six rupees for planting paddy. And that's only from eight in the morning to one in the afternoon. But here, labourers begin as early as seven in the morning and work till evening falls. Yet, they get only three rupees.'

Paranjothi sat up and addressed Kathamuthu directly, ignoring the tahsildar's presence, 'What is your point? Don't beat around the bush.'

'The cheri people refused to go to work because of poor wages. Therefore the upper castes set fire to the cheri. That's all.' Kathamuthu stopped abruptly, having managed to corner Udayar and the Reddiars into an extremely uncomfortable position. The cheri people looked at him with admiration and appreciation.

'Kathamuthu, don't think that you alone can speak,' Paranjothi responded with a threat in his voice. The tahsildar and the inspector intervened, requesting him to address his problems to them.

'It is totally wrong to say that they stopped working because of poor wages,' said Paranjothi. 'We did not call them for the planting.'

Kathamuthu said, 'Sir, please ask him what is the reason for not calling our people to work?'

Ramalingam replied, 'What's the need for a reason? The Padayachis work for the same wage. People from Senganam, Sirumadal and Arumadal work for the same wage. How come it's not enough for these people?'

'Padayachis and Reddiars will come together to oppose us. Today they have sided with Udayar and Reddiar. Our houses have burned down, and not the Padayachis. Why should we be concerned about how much the Padayachis are paid?'

'Don't accuse us again about the fire. That old woman is blind. Her carelessness caused the fire.'

'I disagree. For the last two years, since her daughter-in-law died, she's done the cooking. If she was so incapable or careless, this would have happened long ago. Why exactly three days after our people stopped going to work? Why don't you tell this story to some castrated fool who might believe you?'

Kathamuthu stood up as though he had had enough of the arguments. Using his toes as if they were tongs, he lifted up his veshti. Without bending he took the edges into his hands, folded the veshti at his thighs and tied it. He then sat down and spoke in a measured tone. 'You say you are innocent. Fine. I have been telling you from the beginning that the relationship between us should not break down. You have to take care of the Harijans as if they are your own children. Seven houses were burned down today. Please collect money and pay a compensation of ten thousand rupees to each family. People here have been working for just three rupees for too long. Prices have gone up. Pay them one more rupee.'

As Kathamuthu concluded his appeal, Rasendran, who had moved close to the panchayat side, asked the tahsildar, 'Sir, can I say something?'

He took Kathamuthu by surprise. The elders murmured, 'When the butter has been churned, this fellow will break the pot!'

Rasendran began, 'It is because we having been begging from them always, they keep testing our weight—'

Pichappillai burst in, 'He is just a young boy. He doesn't know anything.'

Kathamuthu roared at the young man, 'Are you a fool? Because you have learned to read and write doesn't mean that you can speak up in this forum. What do you know? If your mother gives you a plateful, you will eat. If you marry, you will have children. Shut your mouth. I'll knock your teeth, if you don't.'

The men and women of the cheri silenced him. Utterly humiliated, tears sprang up in Rasendran's eyes. He slipped back into the crowd. Sargunam, who had been one of the spectators, walked towards him.

FOURTEEN

Sargunam was Rasendran's cousin. She had come to Puliyur on the eve of the Mariamman festival. She was in the tenth standard, studying in a school in Athur. Her mother's two brothers lived in Puliyur. Rasendran was the son of one of the brothers. His mother had died four or five years ago. After completing his B.A. degree, he had continued to live at home for the past two years. Sargunam could not stay at Rasendran's house—both were young and anything could happen! She was therefore staying with the other brother's family. He had two daughters. His elder daughter Saroja was older than Sargunam. She worked as an agricultural labourer. The younger one, Arputham, was twelve years old.

Sargunam had been trying in vain to meet Rasendran for the past three days. When she visited Rasendran's house, she came to know that he was on guard duty at Thangam's house. How could she speak to him when he was always surrounded by his friends? But her desire to meet him kept increasing. At dawn, on the first day, when Arputham was busy cleaning the cattle shed, she had approached her, 'Arputham, let me come with you when you go to dump the cow dung in the manure pit.'

Arputham responded as if she were a mother of two, 'The whole street will assemble to see you—with your long plait and fashionably tied dhavani! You are an educated girl, why do you want to come to a place that smells of shit?' Later she changed her mind and let Sargunam accompany her to the manure pit.

Arputham, carrying a basket filled with cow dung on her head, walked in the front and Sargunam followed her, playing with a stalk of cholam.

'Where is Thangam's house, Arputham?'

'We'll have to go past her house, I'll point it out to you.'

After crossing the school, Arputham pointed to a hut, identifying it as Thangam's. Sargunam saw Rasendran sleeping outside, with a couple of other young men.

Sargunam's anklet bells tinkled as she walked fast.

One of them got up when he heard anklet bells, but not Rasendran. Sargunam was very disappointed. On their return from the pit she found him still sleeping. Poor Rasendran, he had not got any sleep the previous night.

Sargunam had noted the abundant growth of marudhani shrubs on the fence enclosing the manure pit. After lunch she coaxed Arputham to help her pluck marudhani leaves. Even her mami's question, 'In this hot sun?' was lost on Sargunam. The compulsions of young love drove her out into the noon sun. In her longing to meet Rasendran's eyes and to lose herself in the pleasure of his gaze, she could hardly swallow her food.

A group of young men were sitting outside Thangam's house and playing cards. Rasendran was among them. He had had a bath and worn a clean shirt. He looked relaxed and rested. When he spied Sargunam coming from a distance, he resolutely turned away from that direction, fearing his friends' teasing remarks.

Sargunam's anklet bells raised waves of pleasure in his heart, but he controlled himself and continued to play.

'Hey, it's your athai's daughter, she keeps turning and looking at you!' said Thamizharasan, aiming to provoke him.

A disappointed Sargunam caught up with Arputham who seemed to be in a hurry. She plucked bunches of marudhani flowers and commented, 'If these flowers are tied along with the fragrant marukkozhundu and jasmine, the combination would be lovely.'

'Yes, but where do we find marukkozhundu and jasmine?'

On their way back they saw Rasendran blocking the narrow path, standing in the hot sun.

'Where are you coming from Arputham?'

'We were plucking marudhaani, Anna.'

'When it's so hot?'

'Sargunam insisted,' piped Arputham. Overcome by shyness, Sargunam tugged Arputham's plait.

'Ayyo, Anna, look at what she's doing,' Arputham complained.

'Sargunam.'

Unable to look at him directly, an ecstatic Sargunam sifted through the flowers she had collected in her dhavani.

'Let me see how much you've gathered,' Rasendran approached her.

'I have more than her, see,' Arputham interrupted to show the flowers she had collected in her short skirt.

Sargunam, shocked by the sudden nearness of Rasendran did not even look up. She could not bother to pick up the fallen flower bunches as she mechanically followed Arputham on the path to the cheri.

She turned back to sneak a look at him before the thorn fence hid her view. He waved out to her from under the neem tree, where he stood, holding the flowers she had dropped.

The fragrance of the flowers seeped into her very nerves, causing delightful pain.

Today, when Rasendran was hurt by Kathamuthu's words, she wanted to console him. He looked tired and dirty, having helped put the fire down along with others.

'Why did you come here? We have barely had time to speak since you came. You must come home tomorrow morning. I'll wait for you. If your mami had been alive you could have stayed in my house,' said Rasendran to Sargunam, briefly thinking of his dead mother.

'I'll wait for you…' kept ringing in Sargunam's ears.

FIFTEEN

During a break in the discussion, the upper caste men had conferred with each other and the tahsildar. When Rasendran walked back to the petromax lamp, the panchayat had been called to order and Kathamuthu gave his summation.

'In those days, when the cowherd, a Harijan child, broke a couple of kambu stalks because he was hungry, his Naicker master tied him to a pole and thrashed him. The boy was given cold gruel in the morning. He got his next meal after he returned with the cattle, at about six in the evening. Because he was very hungry he scraped a little from the Naicker's field and he was tied up and beaten for that. The boy urinated and defecated in fear and pain. His father sent him back to work for the Naicker. The father wanted his son to learn his lesson well. Naicker worked him to the bone, but fed him gruel to the fill. The hand that strikes is the hand that embraces. So there have been conflicts before, but they have been resolved—we are one people. Those who bear their suffering in patience will ultimately rule the world,' concluded Kathamuthu.

The tahsildar turned to Paranjothi, 'It's your turn.'

'Ten thousand rupees is too much. We can't afford that. It's unimaginable.'

'How much can you afford?' the tahsildar asked.

Perhaps they had discussed the issue during the break, for Paranjothi Udayar replied, 'Whatsoever is just. We'll abide by your decision.'

'Families whose houses were completely destroyed should get three thousand rupees each. Owners of houses that were partially burned will get one thousand rupees. The daily wage will be increased to three rupees fifty paise. If both parties don't agree to this settlement, the matter will be taken to court. Additionally the government will pay the affected parties some money, according to the rules. Rice and clothes will be distributed. Our sub-collector is camping in Athur and he will ensure that you receive food, clothes and money. Do you agree?'

The inspector who had largely remained silent, even yawning at times, now advised Kathamuthu, 'You had better accept the offer. If you don't, things will drag indefinitely.'

'If the government and the elders have decided, I have no objections. Though, I must say I am not satisfied with the offer.'

Three policemen were detailed to stay behind in the village, while the inspector and the tahsildar left in their jeeps. Kathamuthu was talking to the cheri elders when a message was conveyed that Udayar would like to talk to him.

Kathamuthu and Paranjothi walked towards each other.

'I must take leave now,' said Kathamuthu.

'What's the hurry?'

'Hurry? How can you ask that? It's already two in the morning, tomorrow I have to go to Trichy to meet the Adi-dravidar welfare officer. The Ambedkar Association is organising a procession to the police station. They're demonstrating against police inaction in the Thangam case. I have to—'

Startled, Paranjothi said, 'Kathamuthu, can't we settle the matter in the panchayat? Why should we take a matter concerning a woman to the court?'

'I am very busy. If you can come to Athur, we can hold a panchayat there.'

'Fine. Where shall we have it?'

'At the timber mart next to my house. The shop is closed on Sundays, we could hold the meeting there.' Before he left,

Kathamuthu informed Pichappillai and Sellamuthu about Sunday's panchayat and requested them to be present. Finally he left for Athur seated on a bicycle, again pedalled by someone else.

Arunachala Reddiar, displeased over the decision to raise wages, joined Paranjothi. 'We shouldn't have agreed to higher wages.'

'Don't worry. We'll make them work an extra hour. When we pay more, we have the right to demand more work from them.'

'Why did you agree to paying twenty thousand rupees? That's a lot of money,' muttered Ramalinga Reddiar.

'We haven't given in to Kathamuthu's demands, we have only agreed to the tahsildar's suggestions. Later we'll be able to apply to the tahsildar for permission to cut that huge banyan tree next to the school. The auction proceeds will make up for what we are paying now.'

'Do you think the tahsildar will agree?'

'Why not? We'll say the tree is a danger to the panchayat school. Even at a low estimate, the tree will fetch at least fifteen thousand rupees. Of course, we'll have to pay off the tahsildar.

'And you've been making use of the government land. Officially it is classified as "threshing ground". I found that out from the village registrar. You can apply for the ownership document under a fictitious name.'

'But will they give the document? Do the rules permit that?'

'Why not? Nowadays, people use roads as threshing ground. That piece of land is no longer used. If you apply in the name of one of your labourers, who can object?'

Ramalinga Reddiar made a vow, 'Let everything settle down and we will burn down every hut in the cheri. Who will they complain to about that?'

And so ended the gathering of the panchayat under the tamarind tree.

Those who went back to work the next day planted the seedlings happy at the thought of earning an extra fifty paise for their labour. But their happiness was shortlived. Their supervisors did not allow them to leave the fields even at five in the evening. They stayed back and worked. In continuance with the traditions of the society they lived in, the lower castes had learned to tolerate the intolerable.

Work had begun on building new huts. The smallness of the huts, the fast approaching festival and the enthusiasm of the cheri youth helped speed the construction. Over the next two days the kith and kin of the Puliyur cheri folk began to assemble in their relatives' homes. The festival fair had also begun.

Children roamed through the fair drinking red- and yellow-coloured payasam and sharbath with ice. Adults spent their time buying new clothes, provisions, brooms, turmeric—all the items one could want during festival time.

The threat of a caste clash that had loomed over the village had vanished. On the third day, the sub-collector of Athur, accompanied by the tahsildar and a volunteer from the Red Cross Society, came to Puliyur.

The sub-collector, who was young and new to the job, wanted to have the distribution organised inside the cheri. The tahsildar advised him against that.

'Sir, you can't step in there. It is so dirty. You will be surrounded by pigs.'

'What about the school?'

'Goats and stray dogs sleep on the verandah of the school. Though we instruct the villagers…' the village administrative officer replied.

Finally the sub-collector accepted the suggestion of the tahsildar, and chose the shade of the tamarind tree, the meeting place of the upper and lower castes.

Money, rice, wheat flour and clothes for each family member – as laid down in the government rules – were distributed when the tahsildar read out the victims' names. The Red Cross Society had additionally brought a set of aluminium utensils for each family that had suffered losses.

Anjalai, whose house had been slightly damaged, was on the list of recipients. When her name was read out, she came running. A sari for her, a shirt and veshti for her husband and two hundred rupees in cash were given. It took the photographer some time to frame the sub-collector, the tahsildar and the village administrator along with Anjalai, to his satisfaction. Without a trace of self-consciousness, she snatched the parcel of clothes and cash, and came away smiling inappropriately. All the women present laughed. Pichappillai, reading the expression on the sub-collector's face, hushed them.

As the names were being called out in alphabetical order, Kannamma was getting worried. She fidgeted and whimpered that she was the worst affected and that her name had not been called out yet. People around her tried to explain the order in which the names were being read, but she couldn't accept what they were saying. Her doubts and anxiety were so overwhelming that when her name was finally called out, she burst into tears and fell at the feet of the sub-collector. Eventually her tears dried up and she indulged in dry and noisy sobbing. The sub-collector helped her get up and handed her the parcel.

'Kezhavi, smile for the photograph,' the youngsters poked fun at her.

She couldn't change her mood quickly enough to pose for the photograph. She was still trying to compose a smile on her face when the next name was called. Then Kannamma insisted that she would not move until she had been photographed. The tahsildar and the administrative officer assured her that the photograph had been taken, and asked her to make way for the next person.

After she stepped down, Kannamma asked Pichappillai how much money had been given to Anjalai. Curtly he told her that it was none of her business.

'I just wanted to know,' she said. 'It is not as though I'm going to take it away from her.'

'She was given two hundred rupees. Is that all right with you?'

'My house was burned to the ground. I got only five hundred rupees. Compared to what I lost, she suffered nothing. Yet she got two hundred rupees! It's not fair.'

Pichappillai came down heavily on her. 'What is not fair? Only a few tiles exploded in the Padayachi's house, even he got two hundred rupees because someone lobbied for him. Our people should not lose out, that's why I put her name forward. What's your problem? Won't your cunt stop itching?'

The old woman, Kannamma, cursing the world at large, scuttled away from the crowd.

SIXTEEN

The panchayat meeting was held on Sunday, at Athur, as planned.

Thangam hid herself behind a pillar, her head covered with her sari. She could not understand that her problems had been the beginning but not the cause of the troubles in Puliyur. She did not lift her bent head, convinced that she had been the origin of the conflict. A deep feeling of shame caused her to shed silent tears. She sat through the meeting wiping her continuously flowing tears with the edge of her sari and worrying her toe nails.

Kathamuthu led the panchayat along with the representatives of the Ambedkar Association. From Puliyur, the panchayat had Paranjothi Udayar, Sellamuthu from the cheri and members of Kathamuthu's party. Some of Paranjothi's relatives had also come. His brother Perumal and a servant waited outside.

They spent a few minutes, as a prelude, discussing Tamil Nadu politics. Paranjothi fidgeted, nodding his head without taking part in the discussion. Kathamuthu saw his lack of attention and suggested, 'Shall we begin?' He was focussed and clear about what he wanted from the panchayat, but was keen to know what Paranjothi had in mind.

'Whatever has happened, has happened,' said Paranjothi.

'You are being very casual. She could have been killed!' Kathamuthu answered, forceful from the beginning.

One of the Ambedkar Association representatives, already emotional and excitable, jumped in, 'It's a serious matter and you are responsible for it.'

Kathamuthu pulled him back. He did not want anyone else directly confronting Paranjothi.

'When she was in the hospital, no one went to see her,' Kathamuthu announced, giving the impression that emotions were out of order. He had consumed a moderate amount of alcohol and words were rolling off his tongue with ease.

Hearing him, Thangam wailed aloud.

'Be quiet,' Kathamuthu ordered her. Turning back to Paranjothi he said, 'She is a poor widow with no children; an orphan with no one to take care of her. It is proper that you make her part of your household.'

Though shaken by the suggestion, Paranjothi understood what Kathamuthu was driving at. He too could talk tough. 'Look, Kathamuthu, please talk sense. Let's be quite clear. Yes, I've made a mistake, and I am willing to abide by any fair decision. But if you start talking like that, I had better go to a court.'

'Give her ten or twenty thousand rupees in compensation. Then we'll withdraw the petition, stating that we've reached a settlement.'

'Twenty thousand! My God! How can I give twenty thousand rupees?'

'Okay. Give her at least fifteen thousand.'

'Kathamuthu, don't be so cruel. I told you I made a mistake… '

'Give her ten thousand then. That's final.' Kathamuthu rose and pretended to leave.

Paranjothi called out to his brother Perumal, who came in carrying a bag.

'I've brought cash,' said Paranjothi, offering the money to Kathamuthu.

'Oh no, I won't touch it. Please give it to her. Thangam…'

Thangam remained immobile. 'Subramani, take the money and give it to her,' said Kathamuthu to Subramani who was standing near the door.

Subramani took the bundles from Udayar and placed them on the floor, next to the weeping Thangam. Paranjothi also gave a paltry sum towards the panchayat expenses.

'Stop crying,' scolded Kathamuthu.

~

That night, Kathamuthu had his evening meal in the verandah. Thangam lay curled up in a corner. As Kathamuthu washed his hand in the plate, he queried Thangam in a concerned tone, 'Are you alright now? Have you eaten?'

She got up, pulling her sari around her, 'I'm alright, esaman. I've had some food.'

'Where have you kept the money?'

'I gave it to Kanagavalli akka for safekeeping.'

'What do you plan to do with it?'

Nagamani, who had come to clear up, said, 'Let her do whatever she wants to. Why do you want to know about it?'

'Did I ask you? Shut up and leave!'

'Oh yes, I'll shut up,' said Nagamani with disdain. They could hear her banging utensils in the kitchen.

'Sami, I don't know anything. You must tell me what to do next.'

'Buy a milch animal, a cow or a buffalo, and put the rest of the money in the bank.'

'I'll do exactly as you've suggested.'

After a thoughtful pause, Kathamuthu asked, 'Thangam, will you lend me five thousand rupees? I'll give it back whenever you need it. Will you give me the money?'

'Sami, the entire money is yours. Why ask me? Please take it all.'

'Okay. When are you going to Puliyur?'

'I no longer want to work for a daily wage in somebody's farm. If you can get my share of land through the panchayat, I'll serve you with my life's strength.'

She hesitated, and continued, 'If you can help me get mottankadu I'll cultivate either kambu or cholam and manage my livelihood. For a single woman, how much do I need?'

'Hasn't a panchayat already been held on this issue? What happened?'

'The panchayat decided against me. That was because of my brothers-in-law. If you call for a panchayat again... '

'No, no. Once a panchayat has arrived at a decision, another cannot be called on the same issue. But the aggrieved party can go to court. Are you willing to do that? You'll have to spend a lot of money and the case could drag on for years. You'll have to come to Athur for every hearing.' Kathamuthu peered speculatively into the corner where Thangam was seated.

'That money—isn't it sufficient to fight the case?' she asked naively.

Gowri, overhearing their conversation, wondered whether Thangam would eventually get any money at all for herself. She heard her father calling for her and went to the verandah.

'What's your mother doing?'

'They're both eating, Appa.'

'Sekaran is asleep, take him inside. We need to go to Ananda Store tomorrow after school. I'll be waiting for you there.'

'For a few days there will be special food. Lots of new clothes. It's going to be festival time at home. He's got money.' Gowri rejoiced at the prospect of a new dhavani, though she felt guilty when she remembered to whom the money belonged.

On the following day, Gowri was sitting in the sari section on the second floor of Ananda Textile Emporium.

'Choose two saris for your mothers.'

Gowri asked the shop assistant to unfold a new pile of polyester saris.

'Isn't cotton better?' asked Kathamuthu.

'It's difficult to take care of,' answered Gowri.

'Educated people follow fashion, it's all outward appearance. I don't know where it's going to lead them,' he commented to the shop assistant.

'I too am wearing a polyester veshti. Times are changing,' replied the man.

Gowri selected two saris of the same design in different colours. She chose olive green for the fair-complexioned Kanagavalli and sky blue for the darker Nagamani. There was another biscuit-coloured sari of the same design. Kathamuthu looked at all three and asked the shop assistant to pack them. Gowri was puzzled.

'You've picked out your skirt and dhavani?'

'Yes, Appa. But who is the third sari for?'

'Thangam.'

All the way home, Gowri kept turning over thoughts about her father in her mind.

SEVENTEEN

A festive mood animated the Puliyur cheri. Raw and boiled paddy were hulled separately, the first to make sweet flour, the second for food. If they did not get even one rice meal in the three days of the festival, wouldn't the guests spit on their faces! Only a few households had the special mountain millet, thenai. That golden grain would be soaked and pounded along with jaggery and mixed with carefully collected honey. The god Murugan's favourite food! But how many could afford such a rare variety?

Relatives had arrived from the neighbouring villages of Arumadal, Sirumadal and Athur. It was customary for them to bring rice, paruppu and vegetables, the quantity depending upon what the hosts had given when they had been guests. Those who could not afford rice or paruppu brought ellu, kollu, kadalai, or whatever they could afford.

Saroja and Arputham measured the gifts their guests had brought; they needed to keep an account in order to return the favour. They kept score by marking vertical lines on the large earthen containers. They bustled around, cooking a festival lunch, using the backyard as an open kitchen to cater to their ten guests. Each of them had to grind chillies by turn—as many chillies as the grinding stone could hold.

Rice was boiling in one earthen pot. Meat smeared with turmeric and salt was simmering in another. The rich aroma attracted the children playing nearby.

Saroja's mother kept an eye on the meat and rice while grinding the batter for vadai. Sargunam was assisting her mami.

The gramophone was playing the latest film duets at full volume at the Mariamman temple. A large pandal had been erected before the temple. Two banana trees bearing bunches of bananas served as proud arches at the entrance. Decorative coconut-palm fronds hung from the pandal roof. There were children playing everywhere. An enterprising boy climbed on his brother to reach for the bananas. An older boy grabbed a coconut frond and used it as a whip to chase them both away.

The deity had had her morning bath. Her face was shining from the oil people had applied. She looked strikingly beautiful with blood-red kungumam on her brow and a garland of green leaves and orange marigolds around her neck. She was draped in a blue sari with an inexpensive zari border. The morning offerings of new raw rice and pongal had already been made and the deity was now resting. The afternoon feast and entertainment were yet to happen. The temple chariot would be pulled through all the streets of the cheri the next day. Then there would be feasting with meat and the festival would come to an end. The guests would return to their villages and the hosts to the fields to work.

On the evening of the second day, there would be street dancing that would last until the following morning. The theme of the dance was the disrobing of Draupadi in the Mahabharata. The five brothers married to Draupadi are invited to throw dice with Sakuni. During the course of the game they lose their kingdom and Draupadi. The villain, Duryodana, insults Draupadi and her husbands by removing her sari in public. Finally the god Krishna saves her. The performance would be marked by cultural connotations specific to the village. During the performance in Puliyur, the man in Draupadi's role spent most of his time pulling up his sari to hide his huge false breasts.

Sargunam packed a variety of food items in a tiffin carrier and went to Rasendran's house. In fact, Rasendran had come to his uncle's house earlier that morning to catch a glimpse of Sargunam. But she had been behind the thatched barricade having a bath. So he had returned home disappointed. As soon as she placed the tiffin carrier on the thinnai, Rasendran came out, as though he had been expecting her. The new clothes and the bright red kungumam line on her brow had added brightness to her face.

'Isn't Mama at home?' asked Sargunam, sounding a little hurried.

'No, he's at the Mariamman temple.'

'In that case, I'll leave now.'

'Why?'

She looked at him. Rasendran felt almost intoxicated. 'Come in, Sargunam,' he invited her in.

He hurriedly spread the mat for her. When she sat, her cotton skirt ballooned and whirled like a merry-go-round, and finally settled on the mat. She opened the tiffin carrier, took out a vadai and offered it to him. She expected him to clasp her hand and he expected her to place a piece of the vadai in his mouth. Hesitantly he stretched out his hand to receive the vadai.

'Won't you feed me with rice and meat?'

'Ayye!'

'Why ayye?'

'Ayye...'

'Ayye,' he imitated her.

She raised her hand to seemingly hit him. He caught her hand to stop her. All the problems of the village slipped away...

~

On the last day of the festival, those who could afford it consumed mutton and those who could not ate beef. However, spicy fried pork accompanied by arrack was the festival favourite. Sometimes groups of families got together to buy a pig and share its meat.

The residents of Puliyur cheri's north street had together contributed two hundred and fifty rupees and purchased a pig from Sirumadal. At eight in the morning a man cycled from Sirumadal with the pig gagged and strapped to the carrier. It was squealing so loudly despite the gag that children had gathered to gape at it. Men and women who were out on the streets were astonished by the enormous size of the pig. They shouted to the cyclist, 'Where is the pig from?'

'Sirumadal! Sirumadal!' he announced as he cycled past.

'Where are you taking the pig?' they asked eagerly, hoping to buy some meat.

'North street.'

'Can I get a share?'

'I don't know. You'll have to ask them.'

The cyclist stopped outside Pichappillai's house. Pichappillai was already in his front yard, alerted by the pig's cries from afar.

'It has come. Start grinding the masala,' he ordered his wife. After the all-night street dance, his guests were still sleeping.

He had the pig taken to the empty cattle shed at the end of the street. The families who had banded together to buy the pig turned up carrying a variety of vessels. The meat would be divided equally between the eleven families present.

The pig, beaten with a stout stick, screamed and collapsed. The men heaped hay on top of the pig and set it on fire. They turned the pig from side to side so that only the hair singed, and not the skin. The pig struggled, but before long it lay limp and still.

Someone brought the wooden plank that served as a door in Pichappillai's house. They pulled the pig off the pyre and placed it on the plank. Buckets of water were poured on it, and turmeric and salt were applied. Then the carcass was washed thoroughly and the experts with sharp knives set to work. The sliced meat came away, oily and fresh, placed alternately as layers of lean meat and fat. Representatives of the eleven families who stood around watching were first shown the boneless prime meat, then the meat with bones, and then the meat with skin. They checked everything carefully to make sure that they were getting their fair share and at times put in their bids for special parts and organs like the liver. The man in charge of dividing the meat wore only a mini-veshti. He kept asking, 'Is it okay? If you are not satisfied, say so.' He knew that there had been similar occasions when people had ended up stabbing each other with butchering knives.

The smell of fresh blood and liquor swamped the place. The afternoon dissolved in fried chilli pork and arrack.

People were crushed against one another on the evening bus to Athur. Many were going to the cinema at Athur. Pichappillai was in the crowd, carrying a container of chilli pork for Kathamuthu's family. The mildly intoxicated Pichapillai was happy to see the Puliyur cheri residents enjoying themselves.

Festivals, marriages and love struck like lightning and vanished amidst agricultural labour, inadequate wages, domestic squabbles, street fights, relationships and hostilities. Puliyur cheri had settled back into its earlier routine—the daily masala of sorrows and joys. Only educated youth like Rasendran found the situation regrettable. They chafed at the cruelty of caste and unfair wages. This made them determined to leave the village as soon as they got jobs.

Worse atrocities might yet take place in the history of Puliyur. Those might add twenty-five or fifty paise to the labourers' wages. Someone like Kathamuthu could ensure a hike of one whole rupee. Nothing more. What did the future bode for the generation of Kathamuthu's children?

EIGHTEEN

A few days later, Thangam's land dispute case was taken to court. She followed Kathamuthu to the various government offices and the court. After the panchayat, she did not return to Puliyur. When she was not busy with her court appearances, she worked on Kathamuthu's land.

Whenever she remembered her life in Puliyur, she wept. She equated the incident in the sugarcane field with the repulsive experience of stepping on shit while walking on a riverbank. She could not recover easily from the troubles she had suffered. The shock of being dragged out by her hair in the middle of the night to be beaten up like an animal had affected her mind deeply. She would gasp awake at night at the slightest sound.

She hated the memory of Udayar's sexual use of her body. Once she used to plait her long hair, but she no longer bothered with that. She pinned it up without any care and covered her head with her sari. When she saw Gowri plaiting her hair, wearing jasmine, painting a perfect circle of red kungumam on her brow and humming along with duets broadcast on the radio, a lightness spread through Thangam's body. But the feeling almost immediately hardened.

Kanagavalli and Nagamani became accustomed to having Thangam in the house. After lunch, they sat together in the coconut grove chewing betel leaves and chatting. They no longer served her leftover food. She ate what they ate.

'Well, she's not eating for nothing. She has given us ten thousand rupees and she slogs for us,' said Kathamuthu, when he saw Thangam eating on the verandah whilst his wives ate inside the house.

When Thangam went in for a second helping, Kanagavalli said, 'That man is getting annoyed with us. Why don't you sit here and eat.' After that, when they ate together, they handed the dishes to Thangam so that she could help herself. Sometimes she served them.

Her settled life and regular meals began to show on Thangam. The Sunday meat lunches added a glow to her skin. Kathamuthu bought her more polyester saris to wear when she accompanied him to court. As the days passed, she began to imitate Gowri, changing her hairstyle and taking care of her appearance. After all, she was still young, and could make herself attractive. The women of the house noticed the changes in her.

Thangam wondered why Nagamani and Kanagavalli dismissed anything Kathamuthu had to say. She felt genuinely angry when one of them made a sarcastic remark about him. 'The serving spoon never knows the taste of curry,' she thought. 'They don't see how even the Udayars and tahsildars bow to him. These women prove the proverb true.'

~

It was Sunday. Kathamuthu came out to the verandah having finished his bath. He saw Subramani standing at the gate.

'Anything special?' he asked, in a tone less harsh than usual.

'No. I just came.'

'Nagamani, Nagamani,' he called out.

Thangam appeared.

'Make two dosas for this fellow.' He looked at her and noticed how soft and glossy her hair appeared after an oil bath.

Subramani half-heartedly refused. But when Thangam brought the dosas, he accepted them. Kathamuthu sat on the verandah to read the newspaper.

'Subramani, take a bag and go to the shop. Why don't you tell him what vegetables you need?' Kathamuthu called out to his wives. Kanagavalli came out with a towel wrapped around her wet hair. She had applied so much turmeric on her face that it appeared yellow.

'Any turmeric left for cooking?' Kathamuthu asked, smiling.

'You don't like anything we do,' she complained. Handing the bag to Subramani, she recited, 'Onion, garlic, tomato, ginger, a bunch of curry leaves, a bunch of coriander leaves...' She paused and reminded Kathamuthu, 'Today's Sunday. Aren't we buying mutton?'

'Oh yes, why not? Your father left ten thousand rupees with me. With that money, you can eat mutton every day,' he teased her.

Kanagavalli shrugged her shoulders and went back inside.

'Some good lady has given us money that you are all enjoying,' he called after her.

Thangam almost burst with pride at his praise. His gratitude made her feel restless. She wondered if she should fall at his feet.

Eventually the smell of mutton curry wafted through the house. Kathamuthu opened his bureau to take out a bottle of brandy. Nagamani came into the room to answer his call.

'Bring three glasses,' he ordered her. As she was leaving he changed his mind and asked her to bring four glasses. 'Foreign brandy,' he told Nagamani as he emptied the bottle into the glasses.

'You finish yours here and take these two for them.'

'For whom?'

'Both the women.'

'This is not right,' she said as she took her glass.

'Who the hell are you to tell me that? Give the brandy to her. If she doesn't want it, you and Kanagavalli can have her share. She has given us ten thousand rupees, and she shouldn't think that we aren't giving her anything. That's all. Without her money, how could I afford foreign liquor?'

The words 'ten thousand rupees' had a magical ring. Nagamani drank the whole glassful in one swallow. She shuddered, the bitter strength surging through her veins.

She took the glasses to the kitchen concealing them from Gowri who was studying in the next room. Sekaran spotted them, 'Chinnamma, what is that? Is it nannari juice?'

'No, it's medicine for your mother,'

Kanagavalli was cooking the mutton curry. She looked up as Nagamani came in, 'What is this?'

'What do you mean?' asked Nagamani.

Kanagavalli rolled her eyes towards Thangam.

'Don't worry. There is one for her too.'

'What is this?' Thangam asked, accepting the glass.

'Drink up and see,' Nagamani's lips curved in a faintly villainous smile.

Thangam smelled the alcohol, 'Sami, I can't drink this. I have no such habit.'

'Nothing will happen. Close your eyes and drink it in one go. Every ache in your body will disappear if you drink this and sleep. I have it once in two months or so for my body pain. That man is not likely to give us this every day.' Kanagavalli gulped down the drink.

Following her example, Thangam closed her eyes and emptied her glass. She felt her pulse rate increase and her eyes water.

'Taste and tell me if the meat is cooked,' Nagamani extended the ladle towards Kanagavalli with a piece of mutton in it.

'No, I'm not going to eat that.'

'Why not?'

'I have not given currency notes.'

'What are you talking about? I don't understand.'

'This morning I asked him if we are having mutton for lunch, and do you know what he had to say? He wanted to know if my father had given ten thousand rupees, for me to ask for mutton. You were having your bath then. I am not devoid of shame—to eat the mutton after what he said!' She began the account in a tone of complaint and ended up crying.

Gowri, made curious by the noise from the kitchen, went in carrying her book. She was startled to see her mother crying. 'Amma, why you are crying? Chinnamma, why is she crying?'

'Nothing. Go back to your room and study,' Nagamani said, smiling.

She scolded Kanagavalli, 'Don't cry. Gowri is upset to see you crying. Why are you blowing it out of proportion?'

Gesturing so that her mother wouldn't see, Gowri asked Nagamani what had gone wrong. Nagamani replied in a similar manner, lifting up her face and putting her thumb into her mouth to mimic drinking.

'Oho. Is that all? Now I understand,' said Gowri.

'What do you understood? I am not so drunk that I am dancing naked!' Kanagavalli retorted.

'Amma, will you please stop. People are starving for food. And here, you drink and start crying. These are strange times indeed.' Gowri turned on her heel and went back to her room.

In a short while Thangam threw up. She lay prostrate in a corner of the kitchen when Kathamuthu came in to enquire about lunch.

Perturbed, he asked, 'Ennadi? What happened to her?'

'It's her first time. Maybe you should not have given her that much. Look at me. I am barely able to speak,' Nagamani stumbled on her words as she served him food.

'Come on, let us all eat together.'

Kanagavalli, eyes closed, stayed where she was, leaning against the kitchen wall. 'Call her,' said Kathamuthu, indicating Kanagavalli.

'She doesn't want to eat,' replied Nagamani.

'Why not?'

'It seems you said something insulting this morning.'

'Where are the children? Have they eaten?'

'They just finished.'

'Hey, woman sitting in the kitchen! Come out!'

'Me?' Kanagavalli said, coming out.

'Come here and sit with me.' She sat close to him.

'Eat,' he said, offering her a piece of meat. She pushed his hand away.

'I am requesting you to eat.' He forced the meat into her mouth.

'She wants to be fed like a child,' Nagamani remarked.

After he had had his lunch and washed his hands, Kathamuthu said to them, 'Why don't you both sleep in my room under the fan? It's hot. You are sweating.' The concern showered on them surprised and pleased them. They followed him, chewing betel leaves. They gave no thought to Thangam who was now lying senseless in the kitchen.

They lay down. Kathamuthu watched until their breathing became rhythmic. Then he went out and bolted the door from outside. From the verandah he could see Sekaran playing with other children in the small playground. He peeped into the room where Gowri had been reading. Her eyes were closed and the book lay half open on her chest. Quietly he closed and bolted her door. He went to the kitchen.

Thangam was still lying down, on her stomach, her hair damp with sweat. Kathamuthu bent down, intoxicated by the alcohol and her posture. 'Why don't you eat something?' he muttered into her ear. She did not answer him. He smoothed her hair and snaked his palms through her armpits and pressed her breasts. She turned over and he fell on her.

'You are like a brother to me...a brother...' she groaned, but her eyes remained shut.

'Okay. Adjust you sari.' He draped it on her.

As he left the kitchen, he heard Gowri's door being rattled. He unbolted it. 'You weren't asleep?' he stammered.

Silently Gowri walked into the kitchen. Thangam wasn't asleep. Her eyes were screwed shut.

'Dogs! Dogs in this house! Shameless as dogs!' Gowri shouted. She went back to her room and locked the door, weeping.

Thangam won her court case and the rights to her land. But she stayed where she was, continuing to live with Kathamuthu.

NINETEEN

Gowri was waiting for the results of her final examinations. Her father's attitude made her uneasy and unhappy. At home, an atmosphere of hostility prevailed. Mutual jealousy precipitated in ugly quarrels between Nagamani and Thangam. Kanagavalli often had to assume the role of a mediator. When they appealed to Kathamuthu, he inevitably decided in Thangam's favour.

Kathamuthu sometimes hit Nagamani so hard that she had to lie down for days together, unable to eat or drink.

Thangam swaggered with newly acquired power. She assumed the responsibility of paying those who worked on Kathamuthu's land; she also received people who came in search of Kathamuthu. Her once bony hips had acquired outward curves, having accumulated layers of flesh.

Gowri was always seen with a book. She hardly spoke to anyone at home other than Sekaran. She was indifferent even to her mother.

'That donkey of ours will go to college if she passes her exams, otherwise let her get married,' Kattamuthu repeated his formula for Gowri to his regular evening visitors.

Gowri was quite nervous, what if she did not pass her exams? Scenes of her marriage ceremony began to float into her dreams. She imagined various faces in the place of the bridegroom. However, when she woke up in the morning she did not remember anyone in particular. But fear of marriage remained. She hated the idea of it.

There was even a marriage proposal during that period. A small crowd had come to her house to ask for her hand in marriage. Gowri was shocked to see the groom when she peeped out through the window. He was that tall man who had been staring at her in a drunken manner when she had gone with her mother and stepmother to a relative's wedding. When her mother had asked for payasam to be served on her leaf, he had sheepishly poured it on Gowri's leaf.

'She is a bit talkative, but very smart,' commented Kathamuthu with his usual insensitivity. 'But if she passes her exams, she will proceed with higher studies, so don't bother coming back. On the other hand, if she fails, her marriage will be conducted on the next auspicious day!' With these words, he ended the discussion on Gowri's marriage. The tall man was rumoured to have promised an offering of one hundred and eight coconuts to the god Pillaiyar if Gowri failed her examinations.

But Gowri, as she had anticipated, passed her examinations.

Finally, the day had come for her to leave for college. She was overwhelmed with happiness. That morning she went to the back yard to bid farewell to the samandhi plants. She went up to the gate and wondered who would water the jasmine creepers. She bade farewell to the stone bench which basked in the setting sun every evening.

She was one among the many young women entering college, filled with dreams and desires. Like her, they were keen to learn, to experience the new and to test even proven fundamentals. Nobody really cared to know who Gowri was. She blended among the many intelligent and attractive young women in the college, and it pleased her. During floods, waters from overflowing wells mingle with the waters of huge water bodies, transgressing their boundaries. Gowri felt that she had crossed over human-made boundaries – her father, her caste and her village – and merged with the ocean of people. But when the rain stops, the floods recede and thorn bushes emerge. Whenever she went back home for the holidays, caste revealed its murderous teeth like an invincible monster.

Gowri, like many other students, felt ashamed to collect the scholarship application form for scheduled caste students from the administrative office of the college. When an announcement was made in class that the scholarship money had arrived and that SC students should sign and collect it at the administrative office, she left the classroom with a few other students, their bodies shrinking in humiliation.

One day, when a student belonging to a backward caste returned after getting the scholarship money, Gowri asked her, 'How much did you get?'

'For you, it is different,' the girl replied.

'Aren't you from a Scheduled caste?' Gowri enquired doubtfully.

'Nonsense! I am a Vanniyakula Kshatriya.'

'If you are not from a Scheduled caste, just say so! Why do you have to prefix a 'nonsense'? Shall I repeat to others what you told me?'

Gowri attempted to argue with her. But the girl left the scene throwing a contemptuous look at Gowri.

The event disturbed Gowri. She wondered how and when she had turned quarrelsome. The girl's lack of reply and implied ridicule pained her.

~

Gowri's cousin Chandran was going to get married. Chandran was Kathamuthu's brother's son. The bride was from Puliyur.

Fortunately the marriage would take place during Gowri's holidays. While in college she went shopping with her friends. She bought stacks of coloured glass bangles, a silk kunjam for her hair, stone-studded jhimkis for her ears, nail polish and kungumam. She wanted to walk into the marriage mandapam in great beauty.

Kathamuthu's elder brother Kalimuthu had run away to Malaysia as a boy, when an agent was recruiting porters for the Penang harbour. He had identified himself as a meat-eating Nadar and married a Thai girl who had been adopted by a Tamil family. Chandran was born to Kalimuthu and his Tamil-speaking Thai wife. When Kathamuthu had casually written, 'I'm struggling to construct a house…' Kalimuthu had immediately sent his brother five hundred Malaysian silvers.

Kathamuthu deliberately wrote about his difficulties to his brother after receiving those five hundred silvers. His sympathetic brother sent him two hundred silvers and three hundred silvers on two separate occasions.

Kalimuthu had developed a taste for crabs, prawns and fried peanuts with nethili fish. He looked prosperous. He had some savings too!

When the news arrived that Kalimuthu's wife had died, Gowri's mother and grandmother hugged each other and cried tearlessly. In Kanagavalli's imagination, her sister-in-law was a bejewelled woman clad in a nylex sari. Gowri's grandmother did not possess Kanagavalli's imagination. She thought of a young relative who had died of abdominal pain. Later, when his mother died, Kalimuthu remembered his motherland and returned to Athur for the first time in twenty years. His back was misshapen from the heavy loads he had carried at the Penang harbour. He had two gold teeth. The sorrow of his loss was visible on his face. He had brought with him a tin of crisp butter biscuits, ovaltine, cans of condensed milk and large cakes of soap. He brought a gold chain of two sovereigns with a tiger-claw pendant for his niece Gowri.

He kept looking at his heavy watch, informing passers-by about the local time in Malaysia, as though he had worked as a governor at Penang.

When he drank the morning tea carelessly made by Kanagavalli, he wondered aloud if it was tea or hot water. He would describe the aromatic drink brewed in Penang with tea leaves and condensed milk. He roamed around Athur wearing a T-shirt with a large Chinese dragon printed on it.

He talked as though he had done nothing in Penang except eat fish, prawn and meat. For the first few days he was fed meat and fish in his brother's house. Later, when fermented leftover rice was served with dried chilli for breakfast, he felt offended. He cursed the whole of India in general, and Tamil Nadu in particular. He expressed his displeasure of unclean surroundings. He slowly spent his savings on meat dishes at eateries. His clothes were dazzling and his hair neatly combed with perfumed oil. His appearance was a source of irritation to Kathamuthu.

Finally, he confronted Kalimuthu, 'When do you plan to return to Malaysia?'

Kalimuthu who had occupied Kathamuthu's seat in the verandah, answered sipping his tea, 'Never!'

'Why never?'

'I don't feel like going back.'

'What's the reason?'

'I want to remain here in my motherland.'

'What for? Is there any hidden treasure here?'

'I ran away to Malaysia when I was a boy. Look at my misshapen back. I have carried so much weight. Do you want my son also to suffer like me? He is not good at his studies. We have land here. I want to farm the land. It sounds like you want to push me out by my neck! I have lost my mother and my wife, do you want me to lose my son too?' Kalimuthu lamented.

Kathamuthu was confused. How could he share the land that he had reclaimed and cultivated for the past twenty years?

From that day, he began scheming to get his relatives' support. He called them to his house in the evening when his brother was away and paid lavish attention to them with arrack and fried mutton. He also fabricated a story around his brother's visit to India—that Kalimuthu had fled from Malaysia to escape criminal prosecution and arrest. The relatives competed with each other in drinking and nodding their heads to Kathamuthu's allegations. It appeared as though they had been longing for a quarrel to take place. Moreover they were jealous of Kalimuthu's gold teeth and Chinese dragon. They believed Kathamuthu's stories more firmly than Kathamuthu himself. As days passed, the crime supposedly committed by Kalimuthu had metamorphosed into a murder and consequently, he had fled from death by hanging, not arrest.

When Kalimuthu heard about the rumours circulating about him, he brushed them aside and trusted his brother completely. His twenty-year stay in Malaysia had cut him off completely from local realities.

Kathamuthu's fear grew as his attempts to quarrel with his brother and send him back to Malaysia failed miserably. Kalimuthu continued to shower affection on Kathamuthu.

One evening, Kathamuthu pretended to be more drunk than he actually was and shouted for his wives Kanagavalli and Nagamani. They rushed out in fear.

'Where's my food?'

'I'll bring it right away,' said Nagamani, hurrying towards the kitchen.

'The useless men in this house have eaten before I've had my food!'

Kalimuthu innocently asked him, 'Are you okay?'

'You and your son have had your food, haven't you?'

Kalimuthu's son was asleep inside the house. 'Don't shout. Why don't you go to bed?'

'Do you think I am drunk and therefore shouting? For twenty years, you earned money in Malaysia, did you ever think about your mother? Did you care to find out whether she was alive or dead? Or whether your brother was alive or dead, for that matter? Did you ever think of me, my wife and children? Or whether the rains had failed? Did you bother to find out if the harvest had been good or bad? Whether we had survived the famine? You were never worried about us. You ate fish and meat to your heart's content! Why do you think of us now?'

The eighteen-year-old Chandran woke up from his sleep and came out to the verandah.

'Go back to sleep,' said Kalimuthu to his son.

Kathamuthu, fearing that his efforts so far would not succeed, wondered how to be more offensive. 'You can't think of going back to Malaysia, because you have come here only to get married again after murdering your wife! So how can you go back?'

Kathamuthu congratulated himself for possessing a quick and fertile imagination.

'Dey, don't talk like that!' Kalimuthu was shattered.

'I'm not the only one talking, the whole village is talking about it!'

'You instigated them!'

'Look at that! And I have been feeding you and your grown-up son all these days! Hit me on my head with your chappal, Kalimuthu.'

'This house doesn't belong only to you, this is our grandfather's land,' intervened Chandran.

Kathamuthu leaped at Chandran, 'What did you say?' He punched the boy hard on his face. Blood poured from Chandran's nose.

'Ayyo Sivane...'

Kanagavalli and Nagamani grabbed hold of Kathamuthu and struggled to keep him under control.

Kalimuthu made use of the moment to clutch Kathamuthu by his hair and shake him vigorously. The neighbours gathered as nasty and vulgar words were loudly exchanged on both sides.

Kalimuthu and Chandran were on top of Kathamuthu. Unable to comprehend the situation, Gowri bit Kalimuthu on his thigh, with her rather sharp teeth, in order to free her father. Kalimuthu yelped and loosened his grip on his brother.

'Get out of this house, you ungrateful dog!'

'You are the ungrateful dog.'

'You murderer!'

'Murderer.'

'You womaniser!'

'You are the womaniser.'

'You thief!'

'Thief.'

As Kathamuthu screamed at his brother, Kalimuthu apart from being stunned by the situation, also began to fear those who had gathered in support of the former. He parroted Kathamuthu's abuse half-heartedly, unable to express what he actually felt.

'If you have any shame left, you will leave this house at once.'

'Why don't you leave this house?'

When Kalimuthu who had returned home after twenty years asked Kathamuthu who had lived there all his life to leave, Nagamani and Kanagavalli rose together against him. They lost all sense of proportion and showered Kalimuthu with abuse in completely repulsive language. The worn-out broom, broken chappals and all the dirt that passed out from the various apertures of the body figured in their words; words that materialised from their mouths like heated weapons.

Kalimuthu could tolerate his brother's insults; but he found the abuse hurled by his brother's wives intolerable. Chandran and Kalimuthu left the house immediately. Kalimuthu stopped at the end the road, took a handful of the soil and flung it, cursing Kathamuthu.

Even after half an hour, Kathamuthu was fuming. In his usual style, he described the circumstances leading to the quarrel with his brother to the crowd gathered at his doorstep. His words and actions hardly matched.

'He flaunts a wrist watch, a snake picture on his shirt and a minor chain, and loiters about leering at the women of this house. Am I crazy to keep such a man in the house?'

Nagamani recollected her association with Kalimuthu. Though she could not recall any incident carrying even a trace of Kathamuthu's accusation, she decided, 'Who knows? He understands his brother well, so it must be true!'

'He has not given a single paisa since he landed. We sustain ourselves with gruel, while he consumes mutton and chicken every day in some hotel or the other. Is that not injustice? You go back to Malaysia and eat all the mutton and chicken you want over there, who is going to care about that? And why do you need scented soap?'

'He drinks Ovaltine in the morning. Can I afford that for my children? Is this proper?' Kathamuthu asked pathetically.

The crowd was confused, wondering whether it ought to take pity on Kalimuthu who was standing and shedding silent tears under the tamarind tree with his son, or believe Kathamuthu's version of the story. They finally dispersed when Kathamuthu raised his voice and sent them away.

Gowri gazed through the window at her periappa and Chandran. Her legs were still trembling. She recalled scenes—of blood oozing from Chandran's nose, her periappa shaking her father by his hair, she biting her periappa. Feelings of fear, helplessness, anger and sympathy welled up all at once and confused her.

Gowri came to know from her cousin Chandran, on her way to school, that he and his father had rented a house in the cheri for twenty-five rupees.

Approximately a month after the incident, a panchayat was assembled. Kalimuthu had demanded the division of the property, so Kathamuthu had requested for a panchayat to be convened.

'I want half the house!' Kalimuthu clarified his demand before the panchayat at the first possible opportunity.

'So, you struggled hard, examined each brick and purchased cart loads of cement and sand?' Kathamuthu's retort was accompanied by an obscene gesture.

'Why do you address me, when I have decided not to see your face for the rest of my life? Address the panchayat with whatever you have to say!' Kalimuthu then turned to the panchayat members and said, 'I am declaring this in the panchayat. The land belongs to me. Before it was partitioned he had constructed this house. Therefore, I can rightfully claim half of it. Further, I had sent a thousand silvers, that is, five thousand rupees, when he wrote to me about struggling to construct this house.'

'A thousand silvers? Dey, don't lie, when did you send them?'

On hearing his brother's blatant denial, Kalimuthu gritted his teeth. He stood up staring, expressing helplessness. 'Oh god!' he called for divine intervention. He dusted his thundu, draped it back on his right shoulder and said, 'Dey, god will pay you what you deserve,' and started to walk out. But the panchayat members prevented him from leaving. He came back to his seat with an expression indicating that he would not open his mouth at any cost.

'Okay, assuming that he had sent five thousand rupees – I swear, he did not sent any money – what of the twenty years that I have toiled on the land? I had planted coconut trees, and mango and drumstick trees! When our mother died, he did not come from Malaysia to perform even the last rites. When she had suffered a paralytic stroke, my wife looked after her, from escorting her to piss to giving her a bath! When she was bedridden, I spent hundreds of rupees. From the moment she died, till her body was removed from the house, I spent one thousand rupees. Did he send bundles of money on such occasions? It is four months since he came back from Malaysia with his son. For three months, I fed them with mutton and chicken. Will this be brought to account?

You don't think much of this panchayat, that's why you have decided to shamelessly tell lies!'

'You liar, when you wrote to me that you are going to be married, I sent fifty silvers. I always sent clothes and saris for you and our mother and your wife whenever someone came to India. Besides sending money for constructing the house, I sent fifty silvers for the housewarming ceremony. I also sent fifty silvers for the consecration ceremony for our temple. When our mother passed away, I could come only after a year and I gave you five hundred rupees at that time. I had given your daughter a gift of a two-sovereign gold chain with a tiger-claw pendant. I don't deny that you treated me with mutton and fish dishes, but I bought all the groceries as long as I had money in hand. Why did I do all this? Because you are my younger brother and I needed you. But you threw me out of the house...'

Nagamani and Kanagavalli peeped out frequently from the kitchen as they cooked. But they did not share any comments as they were not on good terms.

Gowri, who had been listening to the panchayat, prompted by reasons best known to her, removed the gold chain with the tiger-claw pendant and placed it on her periappa's lap. Kalimuthu quietly accepted it.

'What are you doing here? Chee!' Kathamuthu got up and landed a strong blow on her back. He was annoyed that he had unnecessarily lost two sovereigns of gold to his brother.

TWENTY

The panchayat decided that a mud house in the cheri should be repaired and handed over to Kalimuthu. Mottankadu, the agricultural land, was to be divided between the brothers. Kathamuthu's machinations had succeeded to some extent. He got to remain in the house that he had built and he retained a substantial share of the land—the part with the well in it. Being defrauded by his brother and his inability to do hard physical labour on his share of the land weakened Kalimuthu considerably. Even his gold tooth had begun to erode.

Chandran joined the rice mill as Mottankadu remained fallow for six months of the year. He narrated the injustice meted out by Kathamuthu to his co-workers; they, in turn, complained about the mill-owner's exploitation. Those were the days when workers unions were becoming popular. The mill-workers too started a rice-mill-workers union. Their first union activity was to collect funds to celebrate ayuda poojai.

They purchased bundles of ornamental colour paper and decorated the factory machines—the cogs, the wheels and even the rubber belts connecting the wheels. The proprietor was thrilled by the enthusiasm of the workers and paid each a bonus of ten rupees. That evening the mill-workers drank two hundred millilitres each at the arrack shop. As the liquor entered their veins and loosened their tongues, they ended up blaming Kattathambi, the union leader, of swindling the money collected for the celebration.

As a result, Chandran, who was the youngest and most energetic among them, was selected as the new leader. Like all new leaders, he too wanted to overhaul the system. He collected a weekly subscription of one rupee from all thirty members and appointed one of his colleagues to maintain the accounts. Chandran and Gandhi were the only two literates in the union, so they decided to teach others to write their own names. As some of the members stopped soon after they learnt to sign their names, Chandran and Gandhi felt wearied by the effort involved in teaching. Mere survival became the principle that guided Chandran and the rest. They were hardly left with any spirit to fight against anything. Cinema attracted their attention more than anything else. They drank a lot of arrack. They were resigned to their fates and nobody even dared to think that their lives could be changed. Utter helplessness and lethargy had engulfed them.

They sometimes thought about their children's future and desired the possibility of a decent life for them. But their wages did not match their desires. Their ambitions for their children remained stunted.

The Sowbagyalakshmi Rice Mill and Ginning Factory had hired daily labourers to work along with their mill-workers for a short season. One day, when the labourers and workers had gathered during a break, standing together in small groups, the first intimations of change struck. The Skylab satellite had spun out of its orbit and was approaching the earth at a terrible speed. People were scared that it would fall on their roofs. Scientists expected it to crash, but were unable to predict when or where it would happen.The newspapers were filled with speculations, stories and photographs of the approaching Skylab. After work, Chandran read the news aloud to his colleagues. The next day, they purchased a *Dinathandi* from the union account. After they read about the Skylab and then had read the film news, they also read a news item about workers in some other rice mill agitating for better wages. They wanted their money's worth from the newspaper and therefore had it read thoroughly.

Maharasa, an unlettered worker, wanted to know from Gandhi as to where exactly in the newspaper the news item about the mill-workers was printed. When Gandhi pointed it out to him, he stared at the text. The letters moved like huge black ants in front of his eyes.

Thus, they started buying newspaper regularly and the educated Chandran became their true leader. Earlier, during breaks, workers would spend their time smoking beedis and murmuring, 'These are difficult times.' Now, on such occasions, a keen observer would have witnessed a behavioural change. The workers chose to say, 'Let us talk about what's happening now, about what we need to do.'

Their concerns had moved on from what was happening to what would be good for them. But the transformation was quite slow in happening. Cinema, politics and the all-pervasive corruption in everyday life had numbed their minds. The rebirth of life and hope was a painfully slow process.

TWENTY-ONE

Elangovan avoided going to Athur by bus after the argument with Lalitha. He had applied for a loan and purchased a bicycle. He therefore cycled to work every day. Though Lalitha understood that Elangovan was making great efforts to keep away from her, her pride prevented her from approaching him.

On days when she did not have tailoring class, Lalitha attended to the household work. Even before she had completed her tailoring course, Lalitha's mother had presented her with a sewing machine. She practised at home with old clothes and other available bits and pieces. She also spent time cutting out models and measurements on paper. Her widowed mother left every day to work on the fields. She refused Lalitha's offers to help, keen that her daughter have a better life than her. Sometimes, Lalitha would watch over the grains left out to dry in the sun. On such occasions, the sweet warmth of the sun, the street empty of people and the resulting loneliness would take her thoughts back to Elangovan again and again. As days passed by, her anger melted and the desire to meet him intensified.

'He did not say that he will chase another woman. He only wanted to know if I would tolerate it. I had unnecessarily dragged caste into the argument...' she repented.

'Didn't I know his caste when I fell in love with him? If I did mind about his caste, how could I be in love with him? How can he not understand that? How many times have I sworn that I would marry only him, even if it meant losing my life! He seems to have forgotten all that. He only remembers what I said about his caste, and that too in a fit of anger.'

'The whole village gossips about me. Kadiresan attributed my behaviour to my being the brat of a widow! They talk ill about my mother too. I endure everything for his sake! He doesn't have to experience any such difficulty, does he?' she attempted to console herself.

These thoughts perturbed her every night. Bus travel became a burden.

Lalitha's mother did not dare question her after that incident that took place on that rainy day.

~

It had been raining stubbornly since morning. The clouds had formed a heavy curtain hiding the light. The previous night's thunder and lightning had put out the street lights. Lalitha had left the house in the morning with an umbrella. A concerned neighbour had warned Lalitha's mother about her daughter's activities, 'He is a Parayan! Be careful.'

Mangalavati had been fuming with anger all day. She wished for the thunder to fall on her head. 'I've pampered her,' she groaned. 'Let her come, I'll break her leg.' Her anger mounted as the evening passed. 'Let her come…let her come…' It was hardly seven in the evening when Lalitha returned, but it looked dark enough to be ten o'clock at night.

As Lalitha entered folding her umbrella, Mangalavati had plucked it from her and attacked her with it. 'You stupid bitch! What are you doing with a Parayan?'

Lalitha fell down to the floor screaming 'Amma!'

'Ayyo, what have I done? Lalitha! Lalitha!' She lifted Lalitha and placed her head on her lap. Lalitha's eyes were rolling uncontrollably in the dull light of the hurricane lamp. Her teeth were clamped shut. Convulsions wracked her body.

'Sami…sami…what has happened to you? My darling,' wept Lalitha's mother bitterly. The neighbours assembled on hearing her.

'What is the matter?'

'I don't know, she appears to be struck by fear. Her nerves are convulsing.'

The Konar poosari was called. He played the udukku and smeared thiruneer and some ointment on her body. Yet her fever came down only after she was given an injection at the hospital the next day.

∿

After that incident, Lalitha would tremble if there was thunder and rain. Her mother trembled more than even Lalitha. She was scared to initiate any talk on her supposed affair with Elangovan.

When Lalitha prepared to leave for her tailoring class after her recovery, her mother warned her gently, 'Be careful, don't create an opportunity for others to talk badly about you.'

Lalitha could not respond as she was already late. In the evening, having had her sukku coffee, she questioned her mother who was kneading rice flour for puttu, 'Why do we have upper and lower castes?'

'Mmm…'

'Amma, scold me if I am wrong. But please answer me.'

'Listen, you are educated, so you are questioning me. I am illiterate, so I have to watch what's happening and listen to what you dictate.'

'Amma, if you have something in your mind, talk to me. If you wish to. It's up to you.'

Lalitha's mother stopped kneading the flour and looked at her, 'So, you asked why there are upper and lower castes. Tell me why are some people rich and some poor? Why are there different colours—black and red?'

'Colours are god's creations. And people are fated to be poor or rich.'

'Now you know why there are upper and lower castes. The Chakkiliyan makes footwear, the Parayan beats the drum, the Vettiyan burns corpses and the Pallan cultivates the land—'

Lalitha interrupted her mother, 'We too cultivate the land. We are also poor. How can our caste be above theirs?'

'It *is* like that, don't question me any more.'

'Amma...?'

'What?'

'Don't be annoyed by what I say...'

'Go ahead,' said Mangalavati, covering the flour with a cloth.

'I'd like to marry someone from a lower caste...'

'Are you crazy? Don't you want us to lead normal lives? Get married to your Parayan and he will stand at the street corner and beat his drum – janjanakku...janakku...janakku – the whole village is going to spit on you.' Mangalavati intended to change Lalitha's mind with her harsh response.

Lalitha could not help laughing when her mother's body shook with the imaginary drumbeat. 'Amma, didn't you like *Thillana Mohanambal* where Sivaji Ganesan played the nadaswaram and Balayya played the mridangam?'

'Stop it, how can you compare the beat of the mridangam with the para-molam?'

'Amma, if you go against my wishes, you will only see my corpse, alright?'

Their dialogues usually closed either with the mother's or the daughter's corpse. However, Lalitha was hopeful of winning over her mother.

She often wondered regretfully how she could have abused Elangovan referring to his caste for a ridiculous reason. Finally, she decided to go to the bank where he worked and apologise to him in person. She found herself waiting for Elangovan at the entrance of the bank the next morning.

Unfortunately, the moment she spotted him, she also found Sabapathy standing next to her. Sabapathy was a young man of her caste.

'What brings you here Lalitha?'

'Just like that, Anna...I've come to meet a friend of mine from the tailoring class.'

Elangovan was locking his bicycle.

'So, here's your friend.'

Lalitha was shocked.

'Elangovan and I are now friends. He told me everything. We have many more friends. Chandran from Athur, our Rasendran, Chellapandi, Thangadurai, your cousin Raju, Konar poosari's son Natarajan – the boy who is studying in college – we are all together.'

Lalitha blinked, 'What do you mean together?'

Sabapathy repeated his riddle, 'We are all together,' and smiled meaningfully at Elangovan who had walked up to them.

Elangovan looked at Lalitha and smiled. There was no need for either to apologise. There was nothing to forgive.

The separation had in fact considerably reduced the distance between them. They felt determined to get married and had decided to set aside the caste feud dividing the village.

TWENTY-TWO

Two years had passed since Kalimuthu's death. When he died, Kathamuthu had stepped forward to take care of the formalities and rituals of the death ceremony. At the burial ground Chandran was struck helpless by grief. He wept, as the corpse was lowered, accusing his father of having orphaned him. Kathamuthu wiped his eyes. Leaving the bright samandhi garlands lying on the grave, the men left the burial ground. Sitting underneath a tamarind tree at the edge of the burial ground, Kathamuthu paid the Vettiyan and the Melakkaran.

The men bathed in the moss-lined well outside the burial ground and dried their veshtis in the breeze by draping them over their heads. Kathamuthu wore his damp veshti and the crowd walked towards Athur, reminiscing about Kalimuthu.

'His days are over. He used to be such a miser. He would not even chase a crow away while he was eating in case he dropped a few grains of rice sticking to his hand. Our ayya died when we were very young. My atha was determined that people should not be able to accuse us of being a widow's out-of-control brats. She would feed us well, but strictly denied snacks between meals. Once when I came back from grazing the cattle, I found him struggling to make snacks from the cholam porridge Atha had left cooking on the fire. I asked him for some and he refused. I threatened to tell Atha, but he retorted that he would beat me up later. I thought I had nothing to lose, so I tried to grab the ladle. But he hugged the hot ladle against his chest and burned himself badly. Today I saw the scar when we were bathing the corpse and remembered that incident. He was such a selfish miser.'

No one enjoyed Kathamuthu's contribution to the conversation. They felt uncomfortable speaking ill of the dead. Kalimuthu may have committed many wrongs, but he was now with god. And they all liked Chandran who was respectful and kind. Even if Kalimuthu had committed murder they would have forgiven him for the sake of Chandran.

Later, some of them advised Chandran, 'Keep your distance from your chithappa Kathamuthu. He's like a scorpion. You never know when you'll be bitten.' On the other hand, some others advised, 'Kathamuthu talks a lot of rubbish, but he is good at heart. You can always go to him for anything you need.'

Chandran was very careful with regard to Kathamuthu. He was neither intimate nor distant. His attitude could be compared to that of water on a lotus leaf. Chandran had changed since his arrival in India. He was no longer the chubby eighteen-year-old with mischievous, darting eyes. He looked dark, strong and lean; his gaze was steady, intelligent and perceptive.

After his father's death, the union became his life. He contacted other mill-workers unions in the surrounding villages. The more he learned, the more he realised that most of the organisations were ridden with infighting and caste divisions. Chandran began to feel that union leaders were emerging as a caste in themselves.

Issues of class and caste were so deeply intermingled that they made him think of those blunt-headed snakes that were like rubber tubes. One could never be sure which end was the head and which end the tail. The problems workers had against the establishment often transformed into caste-related problems. The union's office-bearers were chosen on the basis of caste. Chandran felt like one of the six blind men identifying an elephant. All the same, his popularity grew.

✎

Kathamuthu chose a bride from Puliyur for Chandran. For the past few years he had been finding Chandran's union activities extremely irritating. Chandran had gradually earned the respect and trust of not only the people of his caste, but also of other castes. Kathamuthu wanted to lay claim to that respect and trust by associating himself with Chandran. He did not believe that his time might be over. Neither did people belive that. The drunken verandah panchayats continued to take place. As usual Kathamuthu was busy, running between various government agencies, the police station and the court. Cases were won thanks to his help. He received his share of the spoils of victory. Upper caste men greeted him respectfully at every instance. He had complete confidence in his own ability, and in the unquestionable authority he held over his followers. He did not realise that Chandran had infiltrated his carefully woven political tapestry, with a different warp and weft. Older men continue to bow to Kathamuthu, nodding at his every word. Gratitude defined any interaction with Kathamuthu. Young men questioned Chandran closely. If his arguments were clear and justified, they agreed with him. Their relationship with Chandran was democratic. They interacted as equals.

Kathamuthu manoeuvred and manipulated people and situations. Chandran's associates were critical of such a mode of functioning. Kathamuthu did not know that Chandran had built up a strong team of workers. The former was like a cactus that did not allow any other plant to grow in its vicinity. Chandran nurtured his associates. He was like the banana tree that flourished along with its offspring.

TWENTY-THREE

On the day of Chandran's wedding, Kathamuthu went to the cheri at four in the morning. He intended to summon four able-bodied men to construct the pandal. He was taken aback to see that it had already been erected in front of Chandran's mud house. It had been beautifully decorated with thoranams. The entrance was flanked by banana trees weighed down with fruit and ceremonial pots stacked on top of each other. The tender, golden coconut fronds were swaying in the morning breeze. Women from the cheri were already out carrying pots of water on their heads and their hips, filling the two large containers as though it was their own family wedding.

As soon as they saw Kathamuthu, the women disappeared. The effect of his entry pleased him. 'Chandra. Dey, Chandra.'

'Chandran's gone for his bath. Please come.'

'Dey, Subramani, is that you?'

'Yes, ayya,' replied Subramani, scratching his head.

'You don't come to the house these days. Is this the reason?'

'No, ayya. I've joined the mill.'

'Oh, I see. Okay, I'll talk to you later.'

'I wanted to tell you last week...'

'Who am I that you need to tell me anything?'

Kathamuthu felt depressed by the changes taking place without his knowledge. At the same time he felt reassured by the thought that people like Subramani could hardly affect his position in the community.

Chandran had invited a few of his relatives and all the members of the union. He had also sent invitations to unions and associations in the neighbourhood of Athur. Considerable numbers from the Ambedkar Associations in Puliyur, Sirumadal, Arumadal, Melapuliyur, Kilapuliyur and Esanai showed up for the wedding in Kathamuthu's family. Young men from the cheri – Rasendran, Sellapandi, Elangovan, Thangarasu, Sabapathy, Natarajan – and the Padyachi and Konar communities were also in attendance.

Kathamuthu's wives had left for the Karuppusamy temple the previous night. They were supervising the cooking for the marriage feast. Thangam hadn't come; she had sworn not to look at any face from Puliyur. Gowri had been asked to come directly to the temple house in Puliyur by Kanagavalli and Nagamani. She had begun dressing up early in the morning. She had coloured her fingertips red with marudhani and further beautified her hands with bangles. She wore flowers on her long plait and had applied more kohl than usual, emphasising her eyes. The red silk sari and the bright kungumam on her brow made people take a second look. Most of them had never seen Kathamuthu's house-bound daughter and had not known that she was quite attractive. Perhaps a little too attractive and well-dressed for Puliyur cheri.

The temple of Karuppusamy, the kuladeivam of Kathamuthu's family, was in the fields outside the village, surrounded by a thick grove of palm trees. But at the cheri he had a temple house, cared for by a poosari. The poosari managed the god's properties of land and house. Every year the land attached to the temple house was put up for tenancy, and those who could afford it cultivated the strips they had rented. The income from the tenants was used to maintain the temple house. The poosari, acclaimed as a healer, chanted to Karuppusamy asking the god to drive away evil spirits. Any bride coming to the Puliyur cheri would first visit the temple house, offer her prayers in the direction of the temple, and then step into the groom's house. A small room in the temple house was used as a store for Karuppusamy's silver and brass accessories. The rest of the house and the ground in front of it were used for weddings and other celebratory events. The back yard served as an open kitchen. Those who used the temple house paid eleven rupees to Karuppusamy. (It used to be one rupee a couple of years ago.) In turn, he blessed the newly wed couple and gifted them a piece of cloth.

Chandran went to the back yard to look at the large stoves set up in the open air. His eyes were red, perhaps from lack of sleep the previous night. Kanagavalli chased him away, instructing him to have his bath and change into his wedding clothes.

The women too had had their baths early. With water still dripping from their hair, they busied themselves cutting vegetables and peeling onions. Small children hung on to their mothers. The woman grating coconut gave her son some to taste to stop his wailing. She ate some herself. When she saw Kanagavalli watching, she remarked, 'Oh, it is so hard to chew, we must extract the milk and use it to cook the pumpkin.'

Kanagavalli ignored her and called out, 'The pumpkins need to be chopped. No one's doing that, all of you have crowded around to peel the potatoes!'

Nagamani separated the women into different units. Muthamma, an old woman, said, 'I'm not strong enough to hold a pumpkin. The young women can do that.'

Picking up a potato each, the young women moved off murmuring, 'We don't have ten hands. We can't do all the work at once. Everything has to be attended to in turn.'

The men had taken up their positions near the fire. Rice was being cooked in two huge bronze pots. Paruppu and cabbages were simmering in another. The men moved around ordering the women to bring mustard seeds, salt, oil, peeled garlic—in short, everything they could think of.

'Get out of here! Showing off like you are professionals! You come here saying do this, do that. If you can't keep everything ready, why do you go near the stove? You don't help the women cook in your houses. You won't even bring a pinch of salt if asked. Here, you behave like you are famous cooks. Why don't you ever cook a meal in your own houses?' Muthamma rasped.

'Akka, can you lift this big pot and strain the water from the rice? That's why we're here. Only men can cook for marriages,' retorted Periasamy, a cousin to Muthamma.

'Oh, I see. I didn't know that. When my daughter gave birth I lifted a pot of that size filled with boiling water. Whose help did I command then? On occasions like these, you get a veshti and some money. You don't want the women to take that, that's why you're here! Shall I lift that pot and drain the water?'

'Akka, I shouldn't have opened my mouth to you. Let's get back to work.'

The bride was being taken to the podium where the marriage rites would take place. The women left the cooking area when they heard the molam playing.

The food had been cooked by that time and taken into the temple house. Periasamy was frying the appalams, dipping one after another into the oil. The payasam was still simmering over the glowing embers of charcoal. After making sure that no one was around, Muthamma filled a small bronze container with payasam and gave it to her grandson, instructing him to take it home.

'Aaya, it's very hot,' he complained.

'Don't shout. Take off your shirt and place it underneath the vessel. It won't be too hot to hold then.'

Periasamy gave Muthamma some appalams which she hid in her sari.

Gowri unexpectedly came back to collect the groom's garland which had been left behind. Muthamma stepped forward to greet Kathamuthu's daughter. But her stomach was bulging comically. When Gowri poked it playfully, she heard the appalams cracking and burst into laughter. However, when she thought about the incident later she felt strangely sad.

Kathamuthu did not approve of noisy film songs usually played at full blast on such occasions. So the man in charge of the loudspeakers was fiddling with the mike, his record player switched off. Some of the guests were relieved that there was no deafening music. Others said, 'What kind of a wedding is this, without loudspeakers playing popular melodies?'

Kathamuthu signalled for the drummers to begin playing the molam.

They began their beat, 'Jan…jan…jan…' The drumbeats reverberated throughout the mandapam. Gowri ran up to her mother, 'Amma, why couldn't we have had the mridangam? This is horrible, it sounds as if we are at a funeral.'

'At our marriages we should follow our traditions. Mridangams are for the upper castes, not for us.'

'What a tradition!' Gowri covered both her ears with her hands.

Komedaham Valluvar was seated majestically on the podium, looking like a Brahmin priest. Though Chandran was not keen to have a priest mediating the ceremony, he had given in to Kathamuthu's arrangements. When the priest gave him the thali to tie around the bride's neck, Chandran found himself gazing at her. He had seen her a few times earlier, but at that moment a strange and beautiful emotion swept over him. Having lost his parents and experienced many years of loneliness, he was amazed at the thought of this woman who was going to share his life. The glow of turmeric on her face, the faint perfume of the sirumullai flowers in her hair—he felt proud of her. Standing next to the bride, Gowri helped Chandran tie the knot of the thali. He felt proud of Gowri too. She was one of the very few girls of their caste who had entered college.

While Chandran tied the thali he made a promise to himself that his wife would be an equal partner in the marriage. Pushpam, the bride, felt glad that she was marrying a man who appeared to command love and respect. With the auspicious yellow rice scattered on their hair and clothes, Chandran and Pushpam made a handsome pair.

Azhagesa Perumal, the president of the panchayat union, the lawyer Prasannam, and Naicker of the jewellery shop attended the wedding. Each gave the bridal couple one hundred and one rupees. They went up to Kathamuthu to take leave. He invited them to stay and partake food, but they refused and left. Kathamuthu had not expected them to eat at the wedding and therefore thought nothing of it. He even felt that they were right in refusing the food. He chased away a grubby looking girl playing on the podium. 'Don't fall on the Iyer,' he admonished her.

'Is he a real Brahmin priest?' asked Gowri.

'No, he is a Valluvar,' said Nagamani respectfully. The microphone crackled and someone tapped on it.

'Our dearest friend, president of the Sowbhagyalakshmi Rice Mill and Ginning Factory Workers Union…for his wedding, on behalf of the workers…we present a brass lamp. Though it is brass, it is coming from our golden hearts… ' A worker gave free rein to his flowery vocabulary, to everyone's amusement. Gandhi and a few other workers stood up to hand over the gift. Six or seven others followed him, all making flamboyant speeches and offering gifts.

Kathamuthu objected to this new fashion of making speeches. He stopped the next man who was about to go up on the podium and said, 'There is no need for an elaborate speech. Just give your name and handover the gift. That will do.'

'I don't have any gift. I have written a greeting for the couple and I want to read it out.'

'It's all right. You leave your greeting here. The couple can read it later at leisure.'

'No, I will read it,' the young man insisted.

Kathamuthu was astonished at his temerity, 'Dey, are you new to Athur? Where are you from?'

'Don't use dey.'

'Eley, I am asking you a question. Instead of answering that, you are going on about dey and di. Have you come here to make trouble at the wedding? Be careful…you son of a bitch.'

People gathered around to protect the young man. In unison they asked Kathamuthu, 'What does does it matter to you if he is not from Athur?'

'Eley, are you threatening me? Are you Padayachis trying to cause trouble here?' Kathamuthu shouted, recognising one or two faces.

'Don't separate union members into to Parayan and Padayachi. You should learn to speak with respect,' said the young man who had wanted to read his poem.

Chandran could sense that trouble was brewing. He got up and approached the gathering, 'What's happening Chithappa?'

'Nothing, Chandra, go back to your seat.' The union members coaxed him back to the podium. They told the young man to go ahead and read his poem. Kathamuthu was left trembling in rage.

The young man's greeting was not filled with incongruous superlatives. He merely wished the couple well. Meanwhile Kathamuthu's followers were up in arms. One of them even stepped forward, 'Where are you from? Don't you know who he is? Don't wag your tail here, it'll get separated from your body.'

Chandran approached them and respectfully requested that no one disturb the peace. The guests left the area discussing what had happened. Chandran felt upset by the incident. He requested Gandhi to ensure that people associated with the union ate before they left. Despite the quarrel, Chandran's friends enjoyed the wedding feast. Chandran consoled himself with the thought that Kathamuthu had been taught a lesson.

Nagamani and Kangavalli took the stunned Kathamuthu into a room inside the temple house. After a while he came out, making a show of being unaffected by the incident. He went around ordering the volunteers to spread the banana leaves on which the food would be served. He greeted the guests loudly with false jollity. He managed to put on a brave face, but inside him something had crumbled. He felt unable to deal with what had happened. An invisible current of power seemed to be running out. But words continued to pour out of his mouth.

TWENTY-FOUR

That night, in the Padayachi street in Athur, a heated debate was taking place at Nallasivam Padayachi's house. They were arguing whether union members ought to place caste before union brotherhood. Nallasivam was the mathematics teacher at the Athur high school. A soft-spoken and kind-hearted man, he didn't trouble himself with questions of high philosophy unlike others. He believed in doing service to the community, and for him that meant the Vanniyar community.* He felt that the government provided more than enough support to the Harijans. It was the poor Vanniyars who needed help. Such good intentions ruled his mind.

After summer vacations, he would prepare a list of Vanniyar students who had failed the examinations. He would then collect money from his old students, now in good positions and well-paying jobs. He would use those funds to coach the failed students. The physical education teacher, Dharmaraj, was also a Vanniyar, and he teamed up with Nallasivam to promote the school's Padayachi students. He would coach those students separately before any sports event. They advised Vanniyar parents to pay more attention to their children's studies. Some parents replied, 'Oh, we're always telling them to study. But if they won't study, what can we do? Let them learn the hard way as we had to.'

* The Padayachis prefer to self-identify themselves as Vanniyars.

Nallasivam would become so upset that he would not be able to sleep that night.

At the end of the scholastic year a feast would be hosted in Nallasivam's house for the Vanniyar students leaving school. He would make an inspiring speech, encouraging students to study further, work for the community and prepare to give up their lives for other Vanniyars. A few of the students would succeed in getting good jobs. They would initially remember to send some money to their teacher, and eventually when they forgot to do so, he did not hesitate to remind them with emotion-charged letters.

He did not command great respect in his community, but was considered a 'good man' and people listened to him. Parents who were poor were grateful to him for tutoring their children. But if people who held government jobs saw him on the day they received their salaries, they tried to slip away before he spotted them.

Nallasivam took great pains to gather together those of his former students who were well placed (and were, of course, Vanniyars). When they did manage to meet after days and weeks of preparation, Nallasivam was overwhelmed—so much wealth, power and experience under one roof. They exchanged information. From the data made evident from their individual experiences, it was absolutely clear that in all their work places – be it the government, a private company, or an industry – the Harijans who were below them in the social hierarchy, were above them in the professional ladder and they earned more money. The Vanniyars congregated at Nallasivam's house resented this alleged rise of the lower castes.

Some Vanniyars had begun to wear the sacred thread like the Brahmins. They had attempted to intimidate the lower castes with their upper caste status. But their tactics had not worked, for the food they ate and the clothes they wore were similar to that of the lower castes. They were unable to intimidate with money. The gathering at Nallasivam's house spoke passionately about lower castes grabbing opportunities that were rightfully due to the Vanniyars.

Nallasivam quoted a bloated percentage of Vanniyar population – a figure contrary to the government census data – and thundered that they were not gaining the benefits due to them. Nallasivam emphasised the swift progress of the Harijans—they were probably overtaking the Vanniyars. He referred to the confrontation during Chandran's marriage, 'Where did they find the courage to attack guests at a wedding? It is the work of eighteen per cent reservations, we should ask for thirty per cent.'

Because of his experience in teaching maths, he could sometimes arrange and present data attractively. But sometimes his arguments were absurdly stretched and his listeners found his talk distasteful. For some reason, four young Vanniyar men from Athur – Balraj, Asokan, Manimaran and Umakantan – did not endorse his politics.

Nallasivam had a list of eight reasons as to why people ignored or opposed him:

1. They had been to college.
2. They were Naxalites.
3. They were Gandhians.
4. They were wealthy.
5. They lacked understanding.
6. They were inexperienced.
7. They did not care about the suffering Vanniyar masses.
8. They lived in a fantasy land which had nothing to do with the real world.

He thus slotted his opponents.

For example, when old students did not turn up for the current students' farewell celebrations, he said, 'Oh, they have become officers now. Why do they have to worry about poor students?' When rich Vanniyars were miserly with their donations he said, 'Well, they are rich. They don't care about their brothers who are poor.' If people spoke against caste-based organisations, he termed them Gandhians.

Nallasivam would respond to 'It is wrong to set fire to Harijans' huts,' with 'If you had been in that position, you would have reacted similarly.'

'If Harijans and Vanniyars join hands, a revolution would take place in Tamil Nadu,' elicited 'Be pragmatic. Don't live in a dream world!'

Someone once said to him, 'If you are so concerned about the poor, why don't you join with other poor people and strengthen your activities?' He called that person a Naxalite. He did not hesitate to use the terms that he knew – such as, Marxist, Leninist, Maoist, Naxalite, terrorist, Gandhian – out of context.

The teacher could not decide which of the eight reasons were responsible for the four young men's indifference.

The four actually believed in opposing all arguments. They spent their days at tea shops, drinking tea and smoking, reminiscing about girlfriends from college days, fantasising about their potential armed rebellion against the state of the nation, etc. They were in fact too lazy to even sharpen kitchen knives.

They had held high posts in the students wing of a political party during their college days. They had given speeches at meetings arranged by the party; speeches in which they spoke about principles that they did not practise in their offstage lives. Their speeches had been much appreciated. Eventually when their speeches became just empty words, people stopped listening to them. The four pretended that they were only waiting for the right moment.

They seemed to be in the middle of a forest, shivering in the cold. They were waiting for a forest fire to warm themselves. If someone would gather dry wood and set fire, they would be willing to enjoy the heat. However, they were unwilling to make the slightest effort themselves. Inertia defined their days.

TWENTY-FIVE

With time, leaves become manure for trees. The debate at Nallasivam's house concluded with all of them agreeing that caste took precedence over union brotherhood. The four opposing voices were dismissed as being merely provocative.

In the ten years that followed, stark changes took place. A variety of goods flooded the markets. People earned more; consumerism kept pace with poverty. There were also welcome changes in attitude. People held the government responsible for not providing basic public amenities. Where there was a hole in a tar road people planted rice seedlings to draw attention to it. There were demonstrations every day. The women's movement was active—there had been a procession in which women had walked blindfolded to symbolise the government's blindness with regard to them. Women protested against the practice of dowry. Consumer protection organisations emerged. Regressive aspects were being identified and crushed out of existence. But the world, marching forward in progress, still carried many ugly leftover burdens.

Caste organisations like the Vanniyar sangam that originated in Nallasivam's house were multiplying and replicating like Ravana's many heads. The water droplets appeared to have converged to form a wave that was sweeping through society.

Kathamuthu was like a defanged snake. Gowri was thirty-one. She had continued studying, had done research, received a doctorate, and was now teaching. She had stubbornly refused to marry. Her reasons for her refusal were like blows dealt to Kathamuthu. When he attempted to force her, she stupefied him with her response. 'The sufferings that my mother underwent in her marriage! I don't want to be tortured like her by some man.' She also added, 'Moreover, I need a father who can respect his son-in-law.' This, from the Gowri who used to be scared to stand in front of him! She would fill her plait with flowers, hide from her father and run to school like a hunted creature. She was earning her living now. Her self-confidence had grown in proportion to her independence.

Sekaran who had obeyed all his father's commands had now become an impressive young man. When Kathamuthu tried to exercise control, he was effectively silenced by his son. 'Why don't you at stay home in the evenings? Why are you hanging around with that rogue Chandran?'

Sekaran replied, 'Don't worry, Appa. Unlike some men we know, I am not into collecting wives or hoodwinking the world reciting stories from the Ramayana and the Mahabharata.' Kathamuthu could not but identify who Sekaran was referring to.

Gowri constantly goaded Kanagavalli and Nagamani with talks of women's liberation. However, both women were used to bending to Kathamuthu's demands. They were happy for Gowri, but felt it was too late for them.

Kathamuthu was sitting in the verandah and reading *Dinamani* that morning. He had frittered away his connections by requesting favours for people who had approached him for help. He had not been able to translate his popularity into votes. He had lost twice in the previous elections. He had switched parties during campaign time during the last elections, hoping to gain by it. But he had ultimately lost and now no party was willing to give him a ticket to contest. He had begun to suspect that people exploited his connections and voted for somebody else. He had, in fact, begun to express his hostility out loud.

The newspaper announced the formation of a new party, headed by a famous thespian. Kathamuthu was lost in speculation, having seen the news item. He wondered if he would be able to wangle a ticket from this brand new party. He felt convinced that he might be able to turn his fortunes if he could manage to convince Chandran to campaign for him. He would, of course, pulverize Chandran after he became an MLA.

'The coffee has become cold,' Thangam reminded Kathamuthu.

He lowered the paper and looked at her, 'I'm going to win the next election and become an MLA.'

'Is that so?' Thangam smiled to herself.

'He is going to become a member of the legislative assembly! And then he will cover our necks with gold chains, there's no doubt about that.' Kanagavalli and Nagamani commented to each other, loud enough to reach Kathamuthu's ears.

Kathamuthu chose to ignore them. He was determined to make them eat their words soon enough.

Gowri was in her room, writing something. Sekaran leaned over her shoulder to read aloud, 'An organisation of Scheduled and Backward castes... ' He read the underlined sentence in what seemed to be a lengthy essay.

Gowri turned and smiled at him. 'I'll give it to you after I finish writing. Let me know what you think.'

'Give it to Chandran anna first. He knows how theories can be put to action.'

Sekaran left her to write.

'Gowri.'

'Yes, Amma?'

'Aren't you going to have your bath?'

'I'm coming.'

'Do you know your appa's going to be an MLA after the next election?'

'Don't you have better things to do?'

Gowri came out to the vearndah. Her father was still immersed in the newspaper. The ground beneath his feet was shaking. Earthquakes were emanating and floods were rising to change the very structure of the world. She went past her father who spent his time dreaming of an MLA post.

The jasmine bush hadn't been plucked for days. Withered flowers littered the ground. The flowers that had bloomed that

day were spreading their heady fragrance. Tightly closed new buds
hung in bunches at the tip of every branch. Recognition of the life
force in nature coursed through Gowri. She stood there, rooted by
the thrill of awareness.

BOOK TWO

GOWRI
AUTHOR'S NOTES

ONE

She was at the town mentioned in the novel, the *Grip of Change*. Time destroyed all traces of existence. Burnt bricks remained as meagre evidence of a civilisation that flourished on the banks of the Indus river. Her memories had faded, she only remembered in snatches. She had come to gather information about the author of the *Grip of Change*.

Those images that she had created no longer existed, like the thick blanket of silence that had once covered the small town. Traffic roared past, belching out fumes, blasting at people, ripping the air apart.

The house looked different. There were posters on the compound wall, there was no jasmine creeper with branches curling and intertwining. Neither was there a wild kanakambaram bush blooming in gentle orange. There had never been samandhis in the garden in the back yard mentioned in the novel.

Her family crowded around her as soon as she entered the house. The smallest children had not yet begun to wear clothes; the older ones were all smiles, dressed in rags. The year she wrote the novel she had twelve brothers and sisters, and in turn they had approximately two dozen children. Why were there only two siblings in the novel?

It wasn't yet six in the morning, and the children's unwashed faces bore traces of dry, crusted saliva. They were plunging their hands into her bag, digging around for something to eat.

Amma greeted her lovingly. She felt like weeping in response. Amma smiled at her with tear-filled eyes. The moment – filled with the strangeness and sorrow of humanity – passed quickly.

Pride crept on to Amma's face when they began to discuss the author of the novel, the *Grip of Change*. Her brother's wife looked at her with hatred. Or did she? How can anyone be sure?

In that house, they did not store tea leaves, sugar and milk to prepare tea. A ten-year-old girl stood waiting with a worn container. Amma gave her some money to buy tea, removing it from a knot in her sari.

She was given a full tumbler of tea, and seven or eight members of the family shared the rest.

'You must be tired, you've been on a bus all night. Why don't you rest for a while?'

'No, Amma, I need to go out.'

'Where to, sami?'

'Nowhere particular. To meet classmates, old acquaintances.'

'What about lunch?'

'It'll be evening by the time I get back.'

~

Stepping on to the road, she felt that it was higher than before, perhaps due to continuous addition of gravel. In her school days, she used to run barefoot on the boiling tar. She wondered that no one had bothered to do anything about it.

What was written in the novel was true. The market place was full of noise and activity. Prices had gone up and crowds thronged. Bunches of bananas and chou-chous were lying in heaps, crowding out other vegetables. This was not Tuesday, the day of the weekly fair with farmers from neighbouring villages bringing their fresh produce. The ground where the fair was held was empty but for some scattered vegetable litter. Was it from within her, or from somewhere outside, that she could hear a wordless song? The song seemed to repeat that she desired nothing from anybody. She dismissed the novel and the writing. She scolded someone, 'Saniyane…bitch'. Was she abusing herself or the novelist?

The government hospital was flanked by the market and the burial ground for the upper castes. 'Tell me, in your life and in your death, what did you find out?' she wanted to ask them—the souls of the dead might open up their hearts and tell her the truth.

She could see her periappa at a distance. An ancient man, the last of his generation. Though he was cousin to her mother, she addressed him as thatha. His features were of the original Dravidian cast—the skin, the high cheekbones, the strong teeth. He was the only one in their clan who had read the Puranas in the old script. She felt that he was an enigma, full of undiscovered, amazing mysteries. She was excited, she could easily travel a hundred years into the past. She did not need any complicated time machines. Her periappa had a precious possession, a small rusted trunk containing treasured books that held sketches of one-eyed males and females in profile. She stood squarely before him so that he could not take another step.

'Who is it?' His back was hunched, he had to make an effort to look up. His head trembled due to the strain.

'It's me, Periappa.'

'You...when did you come, my dear?'

'This morning. Come, let's have some tea.'

She helped him settle down comfortably on the bench of the small tea shop. He began to say something, but stopped when she gave a ten-rupee note to pay for the tea. She regretted the momentary disturbance and urged him to talk.

'Oh, even in those days your words were clear and correct.' His speech was clear and correct. 'Do you remember, during school break you would come and ask for five or ten paise. Once you got the money, you'd leave bright and happy, playing with the coin.' Such petty memories. What else was he going to trot out?

'Your Kalimuthu periappan once said that you had stolen a four-anna coin from his pocket. His wife went around announcing that to everyone in the street. I told them, she's just a child.' Is that why Gowri, the girl in the novel, had such a poor opinion of

Kalimuthu periappa? The novelist and the character in the novel, Gowri, must be one and the same person.

'I don't recall that. Did I take money from Kalimuthu periappa's pocket?' she asked in a shocked voice.

'You can't remember that, you were too young. You know, your father Kathamuthu liked me a lot. He would insist that I sit next to him and tell him stories. He had so much love and respect for me.'

In the novel, Gowri's father was never shown expressing respect to elders. In describing Kathamuthu's character, why had she paid so little attention to rudimentary truth?

'Tell me how Gandhari gave birth to a grinding stone that exploded into one hundred children.'

'That's a long story.'

'In one of your Puranic stories, the son wanted to sleep with his mother. What happened then?'

He laughed aloud. 'Oh, you remember that! When the son was on his way to visit a prostitute – that is, his mother – he saw a calf running towards a cow for milk. At the same time, the mother, who was the prostitute, thought of her son whom she had lost when he was a child. The son had grown into a handsome young man who had heard so much about this beautiful prostitute that he could not help but seek her out. When he stood in front of her, the mother felt something strange happening to her body. Milk rushed to her breasts. Her breasts became swollen, her nipples bulged and milk gushed out in a steady stream that wet the son's eyes. His blind desire for sex vanished, like clouds before the rising sun. He fell at her feet. She embraced him and kissed him on his forehead, with the pent-up longing of many years...'

If Kuttaiappan could enthusiastically narrate stories without ever questioning their premises, why did she have to try so hard to justify her work? Look at her! Here she was, analysing her novel, trying to fit all the pieces into logical patterns. To whom did she owe explanations?

TWO

Kuttaiappan's wife, her periamma, was believed to have been a Reddiyar's concubine. She was tall, taller than Kuttaiappan, and standing next to him made her appear slim. She never wore a blouse, but was careful to cover her small breasts with her sari. She came home late every evening, around seven o'clock, after working all day in Reddiyar's fields. Kuttaiappan would have finished most of the evening chores by the time she got back. He would have boiled the paruppu, cut the vegetable and ground the masala. She did the actual cooking, but found fault with everything Kuttaiappan had prepared. His favourite food was thick ragi gruel with kothavarangai, seasoned with small dried fish. She had not seen her periamma ever eating a meal at home. Her mother had mischievously commented that periamma would have eaten the jasmine-white rice served at the Reddiyar's house. Was there a connection between the character Thangam in the *Grip of Change*, who had been Udayar's concubine, and her periamma's relationship with Reddiyar? Udayar was supposed to have raped Thangam. But where was the evidence? The novel derived from the novelist's imagination. She gave Kuttaiappan a ten-rupee note. In an unusual gesture, she bent down to touch his feet.

'My god! My child!' he wept.

∿

She walked around the hospital area. Some of her relatives had died there. The present generation was now going there to deliver babies. One of her aunts had died after a botched abortion. Her intestine had been pulled out accidentally—twenty centimetres of it was seen sticking out through the bleeding vagina. Life had been brutally scraped out of her. A cousin had died in the hospital, an agonising hour after she had swallowed pesticide. An uncle had died at the very entrance of the hospital, taken there after he fell

down from a palm tree. Another had been bitten by a snake, many
children had suffered diarrhoea, others had had lumps oozing pus
and blood removed. Hospital sewage ran thick in the open ditch.
More close to death than to life. The certainty of death and its
calm acceptance could be seen on every face, excluding those
of the hospital workers. Their attention remained focussed on
stealing the food meant for patients.

The mortuary occupied a corner position. There was not even a
suggestion of a breeze, the trees stood still. From the maternity
ward she could hear the cries of newborn babies. What kind of a
world would those beings experience? How much grief and
sorrow would they have to suffer? Prayers meant for them were
usually laced with fatalism, due to a fundamental lack of belief.

She did not meet anyone she knew, or anybody who knew her.
When she wandered out of the hospital, it was close to lunchtime.
Though she wanted to eat at someone's house, she felt reluctant to
barge in just before mealtime. She finished her lunch at a small
mess.

She felt very tired when she returned home. Her family used
low voltage bulbs to save on the electricity, and in the dim light,
she could see that greasy pillows and frayed mats had been laid out
for the children. Their sleeping bodies were covered with an
old sari.

She turned around when she heard 'What have you cooked for
your precious daughter?'

'Where've you been, Anna?'

'Just roaming around the town. I can't go to an office like you,'
replied her brother.

She sat down to help her mother peel onions. The nieces
insisted on helping, 'Leave that to us, Athai. Why should you take
the trouble?'

Her mother was tempted to say, 'How considerate!' but refrained
from spoiling her daughter's brief stay. But her brother was quick

to notice his daughters' unusual courtesy. 'You brats! You never do any work at home. When you see me, you pretend to help your Appayi?'

His mother stopped him from saying anything more. 'That's enough. Don't open your mouth if you don't know how to talk to your grown-up daughters.'

'Appayi, we just finished helping our mother with her cooking. Check with her if you want. Our mother wanted to cook for Athai as well, but you said you were cooking separately for her. Appa is crazy—'

'What do you mean crazy? I'll beat you both with a broomstick!'

'Well, he is crazy. Would a normal person drink his own urine? He hit me so hard last week, look at the bruises! He tried to stop a bus on the road and came home beaten up black and blue by the drivers.' One of them began to cry.

⁓

He had washed himself with water from the tub. He came in to the house humming cheerfully.

'Amma, is the food ready?'

'Why don't you ask your wife? I have cooked a small quantity for your sister. I've only used a quarter measure of rice.'

'Oh, that's more than enough for me.'

'Why don't you leave us now?'

'Okay, I'll come back when the food is ready.'

⁓

'Somebody said he could be cured at Yerawadi. So we took him there and left him in the custody of the temple. Three months later Mallika had come with her husband. She wanted to see her father and I went along with them. There…oh god! He was chained to a pillar in front of the temple. He hadn't been fed— neither food nor water. He was a living skeleton, his hair was long and matted, and full of lice. He had been scratching himself constantly and had bruises and rashes all over his body.' Her mother began to weep even as she spoke.

'We don't know if he really is mad or not. Some days he seems to be all right, but there are times when he walks around naked, screaming things. One day his son attacked him with a piece of wood and he was left bleeding...Mahamayi, what have I done to deserve this?'

'Amma, please don't cry.'

'I have struggled all my life...I can't even end my days in peace...sometimes I feel like taking poison.'

'Amma, why do you talk like this? Please don't cry.'

'He was fine. Someone must have worked some curse on him. That day he touched my feet. His eyes were red, so I did feel suspicious. He told me he was going back to work. He hadn't been to work for four days because he had quarrelled with his boss. The next morning we heard that he was in jail. Your ayya literally flew to the station. He had been battered thoroughly. He had tried to drive a bus parked in the bus stand, so people had got together and beat him up. We don't know what the truth is. But he has been disturbed since then.'

Her mother had only repeated what she already knew.

'Okay, eat now. You must be hungry.'

'Let's eat together.'

Just as one ladle of rice was served on her plate, another plate appeared next to hers...

'Let your sister eat first. I've made only a little.' Her mother called out to the girls, 'Why don't you feed your father?'

'She's cooked the rotten ration rice. Can a sane man eat that? It stinks.' Taking his mother by surprise, he helped himself to all the rice and the sambar too. 'Are you grudging food for your own son?' Smiling, he bolted down the food.

THREE

'Girls, can you bring some rice for your athai? Your appa has eaten what was meant for her.'

The silence pushed her to speculate—why hadn't she written about the mad son and his mother? Why did she have to write about the village, the caste clash, etc? How did the problems of Puliyur cheri become subject matter for the novelist? How does one choose what to omit and what to select? Hadn't the mad elder brother existed even during the time of the novel's conception?

'Eat.'

Wordlessly, she and her mother ate the malodorous rice.

'Some more?'

'No.'

Amma sat chewing her tobacco under the bright, starry sky. The girls had joined them. She laughed.

'What's the matter?'

'Nothing, Ma.'

'Your athai is still the same. She would be reading some book and then you would find her weeping. Now she laughs even without a book.'

Had the novelist's childhood been charred by the burning flames of caste? What had she seen in the light cast by those flames? Her experiences ought to be examined and analysed.

'Are you finding it difficult to sleep?'

She turned aside without answering her mother.

~

She had come back late at night from a party held at a neighbour's farm house, situated far away from the city. She had come back home very late in the night. Early next morning she had received the message that her father was seriously ill. She could barely get up.

'What can I do? It's the hundredth time that he is seriously ill. He will drive us crazy before he actually dies.'

'No, but he really is very ill.'

Time is merciless. He had become a corpse, ridiculing her, hours before she arrived.

~

When her father was elected a member of the legislative assembly in the first general elections, the tahsildar had not offered him a seat when he had entered the man's office. The tahsildar had also insulted her father in the manner in which he had addressed him. After her father left, the tahsildar had apparently grumbled about being forced to treat a Parayan as an equal.

Her father had come home, locked himself in a room and wept. The Thanjavur collector had been his friend. He had consoled her father, 'Are you upset about this? Don't worry, and do as I say. Go to the taluk office, remove your chappal and hit that man with it. Let's see what happens then. You have my support.'

Her father had gone to the tahsildar's office with a gang of men. They had taught the tahsildar a good lesson. 'So you called him a Parayan? You couldn't spare a chair for him?' The tahsildar earned a few blows and her father a morale boost.

'You can't see something like that now. There is no one of your father's kind these days,' said someone who had come to the funeral.

Was there anything she could learn from that incident, she wondered.

She had been active in the students association in college. An oratorical contest had been conducted and she had been in charge of putting together the marks given by three different judges. One of the contestants had wanted to know the marks before the results could be announced. When she had refused to reveal the marks, the contestant had walked away after calling her a 'Scheduled caste bitch'. The contest had nothing to do with the caste system. She was left wondering why men and women of the upper castes were governed so strongly by caste and employed it to abuse others at every possible opportunity. Perhaps the novelist had been affected by such prejudices.

She must have fallen asleep at some point. When she woke up, she saw her mother sitting up and chewing tobacco. She could hear the front yard being sprinkled with water mixed with cow dung.

FOUR

The novelist was sleeping in her room. The milky light of the moon had been gathered into the fiery brilliance of the sun.

She neatened her appearance and set out to the vegetable market with a bag. The bag was heavy even without any vegetables in it. Suddenly she noticed a man with light-coloured eyes, like a cat's, staring at her. Her glare wiped the leer off his face. There was a murderous element in his expression now. There was no time to think. She walked fast, and he followed her. She ran, and he ran too. She crashed into a telephone pole, but managed to avoid falling, and quickly crossed the railway line. A lengthy goods train passed on the track, separating them. She hurried home, he couldn't hurt her now.

She locked the door. Her room had transformed into a dark fathomless cave, like in Sinbad's adventures. It had many doors that she had to close one after another. She came to the last door and was about to close it. That cat-eyed man was standing in the room.

She woke up screaming in her single-room apartment. She looked at her watch, it was already eight in the morning. The dark horror of the dream had seeped into her day. She made herself a cup of plain tea with milk, without adding any flavouring spices—neither ginger, nor cardamom, nor thulasi. There was a knock on the door. She hurried to the bathroom to wash her face. The knocking was repeated, louder than before. Shaken by the noise and the feeling of urgency it conveyed, she opened the door to see a stranger.

The combined pungency of punugu, javvadu and zarda wafted in, ahead of him. She looked at him enquiringly. But he managed to manoeuvre himself into the house. She stood helplessly watching him sit on her big bamboo chair.

'Pappa, don't you recognise me?'

'No.'

'It's not surprising that you don't remember me. I saw you when you were young enough to run about naked.'

She felt nauseated, but the man continued without waiting for her response, indifferent to her look of hatred.

'I've known your father from before you were born. He used to come to me when he had problems. I introduced him to ministers and government officers and sorted out his problems. When he didn't have money, he would put his hand into my shirt pocket and take whatever was there. We were such good friends. Here, take this prasadam from Tirupathi.'

She stretched out her fingers to take it, but dropped the lot before it reached her brow. Yet she brushed an empty finger on her brow.

'Pappa, why do you indulge yourself in writing this and that? With your education, you can step out of the car onto the carpet. Leave all that writing aside.'

She had had enough. 'What's your purpose in coming here?'

'Are you annoyed with me?'

'Why are you here?'

'Your father suggested that I meet you.'

'I don't know you, I don't believe that my father would send a person like you to meet me.'

'He was right. He warned me that you would be rude. He said you are disrespectful. I insisted that I would be able to resolve your problems. You are his daughter, you must have some love for him.'

'This is the first time I've seen you in my life! My father has never mentioned anything about you. And you claim to be close to the family! Please leave.'

Taken aback, he stood up.

'Please.'

He left, muttering to himself.

She felt as though someone had spit phlegm and blood on her face. She had barely gathered her wits after the nightmare when he had disrupted her day. She felt oppressed by anxiety. How was she to escape from her father? From all of them? She wanted to take flight, naked and free.

~

She and her father were walking back from someone's house. Her father and the host had spent a large part of the visit gossiping about a common acquaintance, who was a drunkard according to them.

'Appa, can I ask you something?'

'What?'

'Why did you call Shanmugam a drunkard? Don't you drink?'

Naval fruit nibbled by squirrels lay scattered all over the mud road. The air was filled with bird calls.

'This is a road, had it been home I would have thrashed you.'

Tears filled her eyes, though she was used to his harshness.

'Don't call Shanmugam a drunkard again.'

'Are you advising me, you female donkey? We've lost control over you because you've been staying in a hostel. Do you dare oppose me?' He bent as though to remove his sandals to hit her.

A mud-covered piglet ran behind its mother, trying to keep pace. The mother, with a loose and floppy tummy, indifferent to anything else, sniffed around with a nose that looked like a toppled tumbler.

'Endi, your daughter, the temple cow that you've nurtured, says that I'm a drunkard. Does she know the difference between drinking and getting drunk. Does she pay for my drink? Am I drinking away the money that you and your daughter have earned?'

Her mother violently turned her face away in distaste.

'Careful, I will twist your face into that position permanently. Does your daughter's education feed you with courage? If your daughter is this arrogant, you will have to find some customers for her.'

'Appa!'

'Are you threatening me? Has your throat become large enough for that?'

'Chee.'

'Ey, if you say one word more… '

∽

Recollections caused old wounds to bleed, as though salt had been rubbed on them. She decided to have an oil bath to clear her head. She gently massaged warm coconut oil on her scalp.

On the day of deepavali, a palm full of warm oil would be slapped on her scalp. The women would be busy cooking festival food—idli, vadai and bone curry. Her father would bathe her, pouring water in a steady stream over her head to wash out the siakkai and arappu mixture used to remove the oil and dirt. He would dry her hair, untangling the knots while holding her head on his lap. His fingers were like the teeth of a comb, warmly ploughing through her thick hair. He had loved her. And she had loved her father.

That domestic situation changed when other women, and more children, came and stole his time and strength. The confusion began then…She could, of course, have set aside those negative aspects and made an attempt to look at her father dispassionately.

FIVE

'Amma! Amma! I've scored really high marks this time. Look at my report card.'

'Show it to your father when he comes.'
'Let me see,' her stepbrother splashed some water on it.
'You blind rascal!' She slapped him.
When her father came home she was eating. Her mouth was full of food when he asked her, 'Why did you hit your brother?'
'Why did he splash water on my report card?'
'And if he splashes water?'
'My teacher will punish me, so I will slap him.'
He slapped her so hard that food went flying from her mouth.
'You should fear your father as much as you fear your teacher.'

∾

She had achieved a revenge of sorts in her novel. At the end of her novel, she had reduced her father to a counterfeit coin. She had reduced him into an old man reading a newspaper on an easy chair. She and her cousin had been transformed into revolutionaries. Family squabbles made for restricted politics.

∾

She and her father were travelling by train. A young mother, in western-style clothes, and speaking in a British-sounding accent, flooded the compartment with her noisy talk to her restless son, who rattled around the compartment like a betel nut. The child paid almost no attention to her, and made her run after him, her heavy breasts bouncing under her shirt. She forced biscuits, fruit, vitamins and medicines on him, one after the other. The child consumed everything like it was medicine.

Her father burst out, 'While people in the country are starving, look at her showing off! Enda, can't you sit quietly in one place?'
The mother glared at him.
'Why are you glaring? Are you the only person on this train? Talking aloud, screaming—don't the rest of us look like people to you?' Others in the compartment had been irritated by her attitude. But they had limited themselves to silent curses. How

did he manage to act on his irritation? The mother and son were quiet for the rest of the journey. The passengers had enjoyed the scene created by her father, it had livened up their boring journey. And he had enjoyed the effect he had created. But she had hated attracting unnecessary attention.

~

'I am not going to college.' In a rage she pulled the string of jasmine flowers from her hair and threw it on the ground.

Her mother did her best to soothe her. 'He was mad to have told you that, but don't you behave like him! He doesn't have a paisa in his pocket. He has gone to borrow money for your bus fare and college fees. He will definitely be back.'

'Has the timber depot been shut down, or has the chit company closed? Why isn't there money?'

'The timber consignment has gone, but the payment is yet to come. The chit company was raided because it hasn't been registered.'

'What has he been doing all these days? On the day I'm leaving, he makes some last-minute attempts. He has money to pay for his drinking and not my college fees? And he scolds me for putting these flowers on my hair. Why?'

'Okay, he felt helpless and angry. Where else can he express his anger? Sometimes he tells everyone proudly, "Oh, my daughter, there is no one to match her, she is brilliant." You don't know that.'

'Only you can praise your husband.'

Some rupee notes were flung at her. Her father was back. 'Give her the money. Let her do whatever she wants. Let her buy her stupid bangles or flowers. I don't care. I don't want to fail in my duty.'

~

They stayed in a hotel one night. Around midnight she woke up to see someone attempting to climb into her room. Her screams woke her father and other residents. Finally they settled down to sleep. The next morning she ran behind her father, unable to keep up with him.

'Don't keep stamping on my sandals,' he warned her. They reached the lawyer's house and the lawyer's wife served them coffee.

'Please do namaskaram to amma,' her father told her. She folded her hands, but the coffee was given to her midway through the gesture.

'Your father is struggling hard to pay for your education. Do you know that?' the lawyer queried her.

'Oh, she doesn't know anything. She eats, reads a lot of books and for no reason at all she laughs showing all her teeth. That's all. She knows nothing, don't ask her. I asked her to do namaskaram. Instead of falling at your wife's feet, she just twisted her palms. But she grabbed the coffee and gulped it down, did you notice?'

On their way back, he asked her, 'Don't you have another blouse to wear?'

She wanted to ask, 'What's wrong with my blouse?' Instead, she said, 'Yes, I do.'

'Then why did you wear this? Can't you wear something that covers your back?'

She covered the blouse with the sari.

～

The novelist may have remembered these incidents while writing the novel. She had to provide answers to some questions. Was a polygamous man a sex addict? What was the novelist's opinion on fidelity and morality? Why were her male characters betrayers of women? Disgust seemed to inform her attitude to sex. What was the truth?

Childhood traumas and biased characterisation had resulted in Kathamuthu—the nightmare of the upper castes.

Some facts about Kathamuthu had been selectively omitted. Even when her father had been well off and did not have to engage in physical labour, he had worked on his farm with enthusiasm. He had been a staunch advocate of manual labour. He always collected cow dung on his way back home. He would not allow anyone to stay idle. He had helped establish the first women's hostel in that town, thus encouraging women's education and employment. It had been managed excellently when he had been in charge of its administration for a brief period. He had spent his money conducting cases for the poor. He had believed strongly in helping the needy and feeding the poor.

During his term as an MLA, the rich Arumbavur Gounder had sent him baskets of fruit. Her father had returned the gift.

The author of the *Grip of Change* had constructed an effigy of her father and burned him in her novel. It was the author's perspective rather than the whole truth. She wanted to prove that there was no such thing as the full and complete truth.

SIX

Could a writer avoid subjective conclusions? A careful reading can easily identify the subjective quality with just the changing notations. The character Gowri in the novel, the *Grip of Change*, appeared too good to be true; or else, she had not been drawn with sufficient depth. Gandhi had made an attempt at self-analysis in his book *My Experiments with Truth* after his image as a mahatma had been already consolidated. He had restricted his self-analysis to his private life, not examining his public life and political views, which in turn had concerned many lives. Was it because he feared that his image as a mahatma might be shattered?

What does the *Grip of Change* reflect for its readers? It wasn't simply that the upper castes exploit the lower castes. A lower caste leader might exploit his own people. It is not only upper caste men who prey upon lower caste women. Men like Kathamuthu are perfectly capable of taking advantage of vulnerable women. The overall picture presented by the novel is that rich or poor, upper caste or lower caste, the seeds of corruption exist at all levels.

Did the novelist have to write about the caste system to prove this? If she had really attempted to write about the caste system, she should have talked about equality of opportunity rather than the universality of corruption. She had acted like a self-appointed judge delivering a verdict.

Could the two aspects – her father's polygamy and his coarseness – alone give her the right to judge and condemn him? In the novel, her father intervenes on behalf of a widow. Once he has sorted out her problems he forces her into having sex with him, though she pleads, 'You are like a brother to me.' Did the novelist witness this scene? Or did she hear someone narrate it to her?

～

She was visiting an army border camp on the periphery of Pakistan-occupied Kashmir with her friend Valina. Both of them attended a party. Waiters served alcohol and kebabs to the guests. The two of them stuck to kebabs and soft drinks. After returning to their rooms, though, they tried the gin and tonic from the mini-bar. They argued for a while about its taste—sweet or sour? Finally they concluded that there was nothing great about alcohol. Valina's aunt later informed them that they had consumed so little of it, and that too after eating food, that it had hardly affected them. Her son promised to host them with high-quality booze on his birthday.

The birthday arrived and the two young women stayed back after the party, as planned. Valina's cousin poured out large measures of Royal Salute whiskey for both of them. The young women competed with each other to drink it all up. Drowsiness

overcame Valina, who fell asleep. She went on to have her third
drink. Her head felt heavy, but she finished her glass. Her stomach
heaved, and she vomitted, soiling her clothes and the floor.

Valina's cousin volunteered to clean up the mess. As he wiped
off the vomit on her clothes, although she was feeling faint, she
was conscious of the extra pressure applied on her breasts. He
loosened her clothes under the pretext of rearranging them. She
grasped his hands and prayed to him, 'You are like a brother to
me...you are like a brother to me...' Valina's aunt came in with
a change of clothes. She pushed her son out of the room and
latched the door shut.

~

Nothing in the novel was untrue. But the novel was false, she
felt. Characters were mixed up with events not related to them.
She wanted to share her experiences, but at the same time protect
her own self and identity. The novelist had been saved, but
what about the novel? She raised her hands to cover her face
in shame.

The great Tamil poet Bharati had argued about who is a Brahmin
in *Swadesamitran*. Had he done that unaware of his identity as a
Brahmin? He had refused to call himself a Brahmin. Had he
betrayed his community? While disadvantaged communities had
been fighting for equal opportunities, he had written that people
were not Brahmins and/or non-Brahmins—they were all human
beings. What could have been his motive, making such statements,
in such contexts?

The author of the *Grip of Change* had criticised the leadership
of the Dalits – the lowest of the low – at the point when the Dalit
movement was gaining ground. She had poked fun at the leaders
of Ambedkar Associations in villages just as they were engaged
in consciousness raising. Novels have to be read against the
background of their times. When a great poet like Bharathi could

not bring himself to betray his community, why had she ventured into that arena? Did she place herself above Bharati?

❧

The novelist had to address some starkly direct questions.

'Why didn't you just write about the experiences that affected your life? Why did you have to mock the Dalit leadership?'

'...'

'Silence proves guilt. The shallowness of your thinking, influenced by your childhood memories, is clear. So, step down from the pedestal of the author of "the much talked about novel of the eighties". You are under the illusion that you have created a literary masterpiece. Turn your eyes towards those who applauded your work. They are blessed with the best opportunities that life can bestow and have carefully established themselves in the field of literature. The upper castes hail you because you accepted their rules of the game, and you mistook that as acclaim for your book.'

'...'

'All those who are silent do not make saints. Instead of killing the concept of "Dalit" in their minds, you were eager to project yourself as fair and just. You must speak up now. You must reply to my questions.'

'Yes, I will. You have grossly misunderstood the spirit of the novel. Caste is still an indomitable force, challenging all those who try to break it down. The present leadership lacks spirit and is inadequate. The combined effort of all oppressed castes is necessary; continuous focus on the problem of caste is necessary. Can you deny that the novel was primarily influenced by these concerns?'

'The expressions of your conscious, educated, logical mind are present in the novel, though presented quite poorly. Have you ever thought about your subconscious mind and its contrary thoughts? Your subconscious is evident in the language of your writing—your choice of words, in the construction of your phrases. You carefully guard the image of the upper castes, addressing them with respect through many of your characters. Those who labour for the upper castes are hardly referred to with respect or endowed with any dignity.'

Had she written like that? The novelist had to concede that some of the accusations were true.

'In the name of realism, you begin to believe that you are Gowri, because everyone calls you by that name. You begin to believe that you are a Dalit, because others think you are...'

'At the very beginning of your novel, Kathamuthu is shown standing whereas his second wife is in a supine position. His erect posture suggests his dominance over her. Your subconscious mind thus indicates its thoughts with symbols, metaphors and words. Your subconscious mind addresses the rich with respect and the poor with disrespect. A careful analysis shows that you have followed their rules of the game.'

The novelist had grown weary of the word games, but she did believe what had been said. She began checking her narrative and her choice of words.

'I am going to examine you in such microscopic detail that I will be able to differentiate and count your white and red blood corpuscles.'

Just then, her athai entered the house.

SEVEN

The first time she saw her athai was when her father died. The woman hit her head vigorously with both hands and screamed, 'Thambi! Ayyo thambi!'

She finally decided to find out the precise nature of their relationship. 'Are you really my father's sister?'

'What do you mean? Yes, I am his sister.'

'Were you both born to the same father?'

'We are from the same branch, the same tree. My mother and your father's mother were sisters. And my father and your father's father were brothers. We lived together as a family. I was married at the age of eleven and left for Ceylon. I came back with my son a few years before your father's death.'

'Oh, you are a cousin. How could I have not known my father's sister?'

'These days you say cousin, this and that. Back then we lived together in one family. You didn't know your grandfather. What a man he was—tall as a palm tree, very dark. When he sat down, his knees hid his face, he had such long legs!'

'Why don't you add that when he sat down the bean bag could be seen?' Amma joined in, listening to Athai's story.

'Oh, yes, he had unusually big...' Both laughed till they cried.

'He was so hard working,' Amma continued. 'Four bundles of cattle feed—he would bundle them along with a basket of peerkai and place the heavy load on my head. I'd say, "I am still a child, I can't carry this load!" But he would retort, "Don't fear the weight even before I place it on your head."'

'What did you do with a whole basket of vegetables?'

'Is that a question? The cooked vegetable had to be heaped beside his rice,' Amma opened both her hands wide in the shape of a flower.

'Rice—he would finish a kilo of rice. Sometimes he would leave some rice in his plate so neatly that it looked as if a knife had gone through it. My mother-in-law would later dump it on me. I could never touch that. I'd tell her, "He is your husband, you eat his leftovers, why should I?" She would reply, "It is not as if my husband is sneezing into the food!" But on those three days when I sat outside the house because of my periods, she would manage to mix the leftover rice with the fresh food. I would retch...'

Not to be outdone, Athai also began to narrate her experiences. But she had something more on her mind.

'Your grandmother told me that she would leave her jewellery to me. She died before I returned from Kandy. I asked your father about it. He said that his elder brother had taken everything. When I went to your periappan, he said his younger brother had sold it all. Between the brothers, I didn't get anything. I was cheated.'

'Athai, you said you are of the same blood, but all these years you hardly visited your brother when he was alive.'

'Your father was angry with me because I didn't agree to my son marrying your elder sister. So he was upset and he fought with me. But when I fell sick, he brought me to his house and attended to my health for seven months.' She began to cry.

Athai must have stayed at the house during the period of cold war between the author of the *Grip of Change* and her father.

'Your periappa would go about talking too much. But your appa, that is my thambi, kept to himself. He would eat whatever was put in front of him. He would wear a loincloth and spend his day herding cattle.'

Amma gestured that Athai was lying.

'And then?'

'Then, your father couldn't do much for me. His mother's promise didn't materialise. Now that you are working, you must do something for my grandchildren.'

Amma showed her annoyance by pretending to strike Athai on her head from behind.

'Athai, at this age you are so slim and pretty. You must have been a beauty in your younger days.'

Athai smiled in agreement.

'Her father was fair-skinned. Of the four brothers, three were dark. Only her father had fair skin. In fact, his name was Sengan,' Amma explained.

'You have taken after your appa, you are dark, unlike your amma,' Athai told her.

She continued, her voice dripping pride, 'Your thatha would never allow me to step out of the house. He wanted me to stay home and do the cooking and housework, he did not want me going to the fields. One day I told him that I would go to the fields to cut the grass and sell it with other girls of my age. He agreed half-heartedly. We gathered huge bundles of grass, twelve of us, and carried it to the Gounder's house. I was the last one to come out. That old Gounder tried to lock me in the cattle shed. I pushed him with all my strength and came out shouting "Old rascal!" By the time I reached home I couldn't control my sobs. Your appa too cried along with me, he was a small boy then. When your thatha came home I told him about it. He rushed to the Gounder's house. The Gounder told him that he hadn't known who I was, and that he had made a mistake. Your thatha threatened him with painful consequences and came back.'

Athai completed her story, 'In those days Gounders got away with such cruelty.'

The incident perhaps explained the motivation of Kathamuthu, the protagonist of the *Grip of Change*. In the novel, the widow Thangam is beaten up for sleeping with Udayar. She seeks help and justice from Kathamuthu, a leader of the Parayar community. He concludes that she was subject to a specific kind of violence because she belonged to an oppressed caste. But the novelist had presented it from an entirely different perspective! That Thangam had merely been punished for her immoral behaviour and that Kathamuthu had intervened and succeeded in blowing it up into caste-related violence. The impression created was that the upper castes had handled the incident as a man-versus-woman problem, whereas the lower castes had given it the caste slant. How did the novelist dare to distort history with such impunity?

EIGHT

Amma described her to Athai, 'She was always deep in some book.'

She picked up an old magazine that was lying in the house. It surprised her that she could guess the endings of many of the stories written by popular writers. Why should any story lead to an obvious conclusion? When life was so difficult and complicated, writers set themselves apart and made their stories easy and simple. What kind of writer was Sivakami, the author of the *Grip of Change*?

While the village caste structure was complex – with various internal hierarchies and a myriad restrictions in the interaction between castes – she had divided them, with ease, into the upper castes and the lower castes. In the caste clash, the Vanniyars join with the upper castes in penalising the Dalits. Karl Marx had said 'Workers of the world unite.' The Vanniyars and Dalits are the workers in this society. If they are united then the ensuing revolution would overturn the country. The novelist had been overwhelmed by an ideology that seemed to offer an instant remedy to thousands of years of history. Her imagintion ran wild in placing the Padayachis, who refused to link hands with the Parayars, along with the lower castes as a whole. She blamed the Dalit leader Kathamuthu and the Vanniyar activist Nallasivam for obstruction, and had replaced them with Chandran—young, energetic, committed. She had thus united both communities! There must be a basic flaw in the novelist's makeup for her to have been able to reach such a conclusion. When had the novelist begun to write?

~

The town did not have a pond blooming with lotuses and lilies. But she could enjoy ponds and flowers in her schoolbooks and storybooks. How she had loved the fantasy of books! When she was in class eight, she wrote a historical play promoting world unity. She was careful not to show it to anyone. She wanted to surprise everyone when the play was published to thunderous acclaim. Unfortunately for her, the play was never published. That did not prevent later attempts. While standing in a queue at the flour mill, she read a story about a young man and woman who fell in love with each other and were tragically separated. She shed a lot of tears for those legendary lovers. After that she hummed only sad songs while plucking flowers. Inspired, she wrote two pairs of stories with four pairs of historical lovers. In all those stories, the lovers either parted or died. She showed these stories to her Tamil teacher. She had expected her to be astounded. The teacher was astounded, 'You are hardly twelve! And you're writing about "love"!' She helpfully added, 'Think like a child and act like a child.'

The teacher asked her to write a children's story. So she made an attempt to write something for a children's magazine. She wrote about a stepmother's cruelty. The stepmother pampered her own child while torturing the child of the first wife, who therefore runs away from home. Her stepsister falls very ill…What drama! The Tamil teacher liked the story and recommended its publication in a Christian magazine. The story reached her father. He was furious, 'Why are you clowning about writing stories instead of studying? A cruel stepmother! Your stepmother has been slogging in the kitchen since the day she stepped into this house. You don't do any work, you spend all your time reading storybooks and then *you* write about a stepmother's torture! Shall I send you to work in the fields? Perhaps I should buy some ten goats for you to tend?' Two mangoes hit with one stone—she had provoked her father and published a story.

She was deeply affected by an incident at school. She and Arputharani were punished for being noisy. They were kneeling on the floor. As they were not allowed to talk, they decided to play a game. Arputharani would close her eyes and she would hide a small piece of chalk somewhere on her body. When she was ready, Arputharani would open her eyes and find the chalk. On her part, she demanded that Arputharani find the chalk at first attempt. The first time, she placed the chalk inside her mouth. Her shrewd partner discovered it. The second time she hid it in her hair and her playmate found it immediately. Then she put it inside her ear and Arputharani found it again. But they could not get the chalk out of her ear. They only succeeded in pushing the chalk further inside. It hurt so badly that she began to cry. The whole class and the strict teacher ended up learning about the game. She was taken to the government hospital and the chalk was flushed out of her ear. The incident happened when she was in primary school. In high school she wrote a short narrative based on the game and its consequences. The Tamil teacher again passed it on to the editor of the Christian magazine. The editor asked her a simple question, 'Do you want to become a literary giant, or end up being a small-time writer, writing bits and pieces?'

Writing about one's own experience did not constitute literature. A lotus bloomed in the drying pond, a bee drank the flower's bitter honey and fell in love with it! The beauty of poetry lies in its falsehood! Falsehood was appreciated not only in poetry but also in fiction. Why blame the Tamil teacher and the magazine editor for being terrible influences on her art and craft? Magazines might have refused to publish her writing, but no one had told her to stop writing, had they?

She had been one of the few selected for a short story competition for college students. The students were to produce short stories within three hours of the announcement of the title—'The colour of milk is white'. Who could dispute that? She could do nothing in those three hours except burden the floor with her weight. She closed her eyes to think of something. She could see only mud-brown sheep and black goats in great numbers moving around aimlessly. Phrases like 'sour keerai' and 'cholam' kept wandering into her mind. Blouseless women appeared in rags, an old woman with a bald head, a woman with a bulging stomach, a tuberculosis patient at the hospital – their names would translate as Baldie, Broken Cart and Big Bum – could they become heroines in her short story? She feared she would be condemned if she wrote about them. She could only remember how she had struggled to collect ripe red chillies with the sun blazing over her head. And the bath she once had, substituting clay for soap at the muddy irrigation tank. She doubted whether any of this would interest readers. Even the rhyming words in the 'la' series – kala, kila, vila – were the names of wild berries. She felt that her life, her people and the things she was associated with, were of no value to others. Finally she submitted a blank sheet with just her name written on it.

When she left the hall, she learned something more about story writing. She heard one of the students say, 'I felt all right as soon as I heard the title. The letters added up to nine, my lucky number.'

Where had those wretched romantic and routine poetic words found in great literature disappeared? Why couldn't she remember any of them? When she reached home, she decided to write about Sembattaiyan, the cowherd. She wrote about one day in his life. The story was published in a leading literary weekly.

She received nearly two hundred letters from readers: What is the point of the story? What can you do to remove Sembattaiyan's poverty? What is the benefit of this story to society? Were you in love with this man? Have you ever herded cows?

She trembled at the prospect of being a writer who also had to be a do-gooder and problem-solver. Amidst her daily problems, she had to find a satisfactory conclusion for the story of Sembattaiyan's life.

No wonder writers keep bumping off their characters. She could only resolve Sembattaiyan's story by killing him. A cobra had lain await for him. Among the group of Nallachi, Oothupattarai, Kodukku and Chinnan, the cobra chose Sembattaiyan. The Chandali who killed the stout Sembattaiyan with a snakebite—did anyone care if she wrote at all?

NINE

The novelist had to bend and twist her stories to prescribed endings.

The twists and turns had thus led her away from the field and the forest. Away from the bush and the bird nest. She could have inhaled the fragrance of the rare wild flowers of the forest. The sweet fragrance of those flowers would not have been lost in the chemistry of poetic substances. Those flowers were never to be found again! To look for them, she had to go back to her youth, to those destroyed forests where sunlight danced on plants and creepers, to the chirping of birds, to those thorny shrubs housing their nests, to the speckled eggs—away from the smoke and noise of city streets.

For those pure rain-opened flowers she would have to turn back. She softened in her memories. The scent of the thumbai, the shiny leeches on the heaped cow dung, the solitude of the clear stream...

What is the force that compels the pen forward? Why and how are experiences transmuted in writing? How was the writer to venture in spirit to those places inaccessible to flesh and blood? She felt that she was guided by the reader rather than by her own instinct. At times, both seemed to be the same, until she carefully analysed them. Why did she have to change herself so much to suit the reader? Or was the change a mask that she willingly wore to attract attention?

During the novelist's childhood, her father woke everybody up at five in the morning. She had to reach the field before the stars disappeared into the bright morning sky. They owned a piece of dry land at a short distance from the house. That land had been made suitable for cultivating paddy because a well had been dug recently. Her father insisted that his children work on the farm, though he rarely found the time to do his share. There was work every day—reaping, sowing, removing weeds, feeding the cattle. She was always alert for the coiled krait while gathering bundles of hay. She competed with the boys to carry two bundles instead of one. She would have carried hay back and forth four times when the eight o'clock horn was sounded. But she hated being seen with a bundle of hay on her head by any of her classmates or friends. She took a circuitous route and if she met one of her classmates she pretended that she couldn't see the person because the trailing hay obstructed her vision. Her father had chided her for feeling ashamed about doing work.

~

Why had she longed for good clothes and good food?

The education inspector was to pay a visit to her school.

She wore a faded blue dhavani. She wore it every day, even on holidays when she had to work in the plaintain grove or gather firewood. It had a few holes. But she wore it neatly, hiding them within the folds. However, the headmistress possessed eagle eyes. 'Don't you have another dhavani? You are the school pupil leader! Borrow a dhavani from someone else. Shenbaga, you have many clothes. Take her home and give her a dhavani. Quick.'

They walked in uneasy silence. Shenbaga's father, a Nadar who owned a shop that sold kitchen utensils, stopped her at the gate. Shenbaga went inside and came out immediately. 'My mother says we can't lend you a dhavani. You belong to the Paraya caste…What shall we do?'

She could have confronted the nun. But she went home in a rage. A rage that she could not unleash on her father. She ranted at her mother, 'Your husband has the money to drink and sleep around with women, but he can't spare some for a dhavani? He has fathered a house full of children, why can't he die instead of putting us to such shame? I can't even borrow a piece of cloth because of my caste! I want to kill myself!'

Her father heard all that she had to say. He could not scold her because she was sobbing violently. He was close to tears himself. He spoke to her mother, 'Remove your nose-ring!' The thali had already been pawned. He barked at her, 'Follow me.' She ran behind him. They went to the school with two new dhavanis.

He went up to the nun, 'Look, you collect donations and run this school without getting your clothes dirty. What can you understand of a poor farmer's plight? A faded dhavani will not stop anyone from studying. Teach her to study, don't teach her to whore herself with new clothes. If this girl had jumped into a well, who would have answered for that death? Look at my sandals.' He bent down and removed one, 'They are torn. I don't even have a few annas to repair them! Don't turn me into a maniac!'

She stood in a corner, cringing with fear. He walked out without looking back. Later he could not hold forth on any occasion without referring to the incident of the dhavani. But that is another story.

～

On another occasion, the entire class went to attend the puberty celebrations of Chandrika. The novelist was one of the five lower caste students who were separated from the others when food was served. She found it difficult to eat.

～

She was in the same class as her relative Pachaiammal, who was teased because her name meant 'Mother of Greens'. She was also given nicknames such as 'Sour Greens' and 'Broomstick', because her family sold those commodities in the weekly market. She used castor oil on her hair. Her coiffure was never disturbed even in a strong wind and it emitted a strange odour. This was much discussed at school.

Pachaiammal was once selected to enact a male role in the school play. On stage, instead of saying, 'the woman from Bombay', she said, 'the bitch from Bombay'.

The drama committee decided, 'Lower caste students should not be given roles in school plays.'

Such words had been generously scattered in the novel, the *Grip of Change*. The publishers had carefully removed them so as not to upset their respectable readers.

~

'You have disapproved of drinking and whoring in your novel,' she probed the novelist.

'It's not a novel aimed at freeing people from alcoholism,' snapped the novelist rudely.

'But at every opportunity you condemn it. An upper caste attitude, in fact, to condemn the lower castes for their drinking habits.'

'You want me to say that drinking is bad?'

'You've taken pains to say just that. You fault the lower castes for their lifestyles. You fault them for even living.'

'Don't upper castes drink? Don't they practice polygamy? I have illustrated that too in my novel. I don't only blame the lower castes.'

'You dodge from providing direct answers to my questions.'

'I am not here to lay down rules about drinking. Drinking is fine as long as the drinkers don't make it an excuse for hurting others. As long as people don't drink and throw up on me!'

'So drinking is bad according to you.'

'You keep jumping into conclusions with ease.'
There was silence. The novelist faded out gradually.

TEN

The author of the *Grip of Change* wrote her father a letter.
Distance made that luxury possible, it also inspired sentiments
foreign to her. The conventional beginning 'My dear Appa,'
appeared to bear the true weight of her emotions. She could not
stop words that were alien to her from filling the letter. She hoped
that her father might perceive her in a different light. But a huge
shock awaited her when she went home. Her letter had been read
aloud to many and subjected to ridicule in a manner unique to her
father. Kullan, Kathan, Durairaj vathiyar, Satyamoorthi vaidyar
and Agri Ponnaiah—they had all been able to enjoy her letter.

~

'She would like to serve the people!' As he spoke, everyone
laughed.

'She is going to serve the people without a salary! Say that you
will work for the money you earn. Say that you will be true to your
work. Don't say you are going do service!' Everyone laughed until
they cried.

'If she had said that she would discharge her duties honestly
and sincerely, and help her aging father and financially troubled
family there would be some meaning to her words.'

~

She had cringed with shame. Had she planned to wreak vengeance
on his mockery? His taunts, jibes, sneers? Is that why she wrote of
her father as a fraud who used his commitment to serve the poor
as a facade to line his own pockets?

In her novel she had painted Kathamuthu as a villain who had taken the money that belonged to Thangam. But in real life, her father had been a benevolent man. He had been kind to the poor. When they came with petitions for help, he had fed them with whatever he could afford. Perhaps the character Kathamuthu was not based on her father? Could it be that the character was drawn from her general impression of politicians who took bribes even from their poor constituents? Irrespective of whether Kathamuthu was based on her father or not, was she an ideal person?

~

'So you wanted to serve the people. How is that working?'

'You can't underestimate my life, you know that.'

'Please don't make me a partner in your deeds.'

The question made her think. She realised, as her critic expected her to, that she had not done anything noteworthy. Had she ever volunteered to spend time in a hospital with patients? Had she nursed the wounded soldiers of her country? Had she taught vocational crafts to children during her holidays? What kind of service could she have performed? Did she think that filling pages with her writing constituted social service?

The novelist was ready with her answer.

'If I go to a hospital, I can't bear to see people suffering. You won't believe how hard I have cried. When I travel by rickshaw, I have always felt sorry for the rickshaw puller. In fact, I wrote about Sembattaiyan's plight only after I had wept for him.'

'So you felt sorry for the rickshaw puller. But when he demanded more money than you had agreed to pay, didn't you burst with righteous anger?'

Visibly annoyed, the novelist replied, 'The rickshaw puller's fare and his honesty are issues unconnected to this literary discussion. The point is, I empathised with him.'

'You fail to see the connection?'

'...'

'Why are you silent? Your beliefs and actions don't match. As an author, don't you think that your life should be true to your writing? If it is not, then writing is just a skill to earn money or reputation.'

'I lead a simple life. I do my own work. I help people when I'm able to. I am polite and courteous to all. And I always feel the need to do something for people.'

'Ah! A humane life is a service to the people indeed!'

The novelist felt that the time had come to question her critic, 'You have taunted me successfully. What service do you do?'

'I am a reviewer, a critic. I am the one who asks questions. To the readers you are dead. I have brought you back to life. Let that inform your attitude.'

'You say that I have critiqued my father. How are you different from me? Have you spun out of the solar system that you cannot be assessed by common standards? I try to assist those who seek my help. I only travel by second class. On holidays I do agricultural work. I gave away all the gifts that I had received, once...What about you?'

'Why have you stopped? You attempt to hide your faults by listing the faults of those who dare criticise you.'

~

'Gudees...gudees...gudees...'

Someone was singing for the pigs. A whole herd of them ran, their tails twitching, to noisily drink water from the shallow wooden tub.

Amma had hung the pork curry in a pot from the rafter for twelve days. The children had gathered around, waiting eagerly. She had not served them the dish, waiting for her husband who was out of town. When it was no longer possible to let it ferment she took it down. The curry had bubbled and foamed to a sour mess. The novelist and her siblings had to take it to the field to throw it away. Their science textbooks said pork meat bred tapeworms in your stomach.

~

'That is certainly a Brahminical opinion. Now you want people who eat pork to convert and civilise themselves.'

ELEVEN

She was sprinkling water on the front yard when two people went past her into the house carrying her brother. She rushed after them in a panic.
'He had hung himself from a tree. If we hadn't found him he would have been dead in a few minutes.' His throat had rope burns. The family's attention was focussed on him for the whole day. He was studying in seventh standard then.
Within a few days of his suicide attempt he stole forty rupees and ran away from home. He came back after a few days. He was scolded when he left. He was scolded when he came back.

~

He caught water snakes and scared the family. He lay in wait for cobras and kraits in shrubs and bushes. When that bored him he lay flat on a bicycle and rode it.
He chose to work because he couldn't study. Later choice became compulsion. Their father wanted him to wake up at four in the morning. But he kept snoozing until it was five thirty. By the time he provided water for the cattle and started for the field, it was usually six in the morning. He would nap underneath a tree and finally begin work at eight.
She sometimes took food for him. She would just call out 'Food!' to him. He never replied.

~

When he and two other boys of his age stood chatting near the fence, she was climbing a neem tree.

'Why are you climbing up the tree like a monkey?' She pretended not to hear him and continued to climb.

'Get down.'

'How does it bother you if I climb a tree?'

He hit her and she went crying to her mother, who scolded both of them.

~

He climbed coconut trees, plucked bunches of fruit, removed the husk and sold the coconut, keeping the money for himself. If he was asked to pluck a single coconut for the kitchen, he refused. Even if he did climb the tree and pluck a coconut, he would not remove the husk. Her mother would have to huff and puff with a kitchen knife.

~

The harvested paddy had already been sent home. She gathered the broom, the large sieve, etc and was preparing to leave. He stopped her, 'Stop. I want to ask you something.'

She stopped reluctantly.

'Did you see Rangasamy and Saroja together?'

'Saroja was serving food to Rangasamy inside her house. Saroja's mother was sitting outside. That's all.'

'Is that all you saw?' He hesitated and left.

She wondered, 'Was that all? I saw Rangasamy brushing against Saroja's dhavani on the bus. And she did not move at all. And she was serving food to him as if he was her husband. How can you say that it doesn't mean anything? I peeked into the house and ran away. But I warned her mother—you let a young woman serve that man food while you sit outside? She accused me of creating rumours. But I saw what I saw. Rangasamy is a married man.

What if something happens? How am I wrong in asking Saroja's mother about it? How did he get to know about it?'

But really. The novelist does not have to police the community. If people brush against each other, how does it matter to her? And she says men should not be served food inside the house! Perhaps she is worried that if Rangasamy takes a second wife, the children of his first wife would suffer.

~

She was home for vacation, and had been provided with the rare opportunity of taking the cattle to graze behind the house. As she slipped into a daydream, the cows strayed into the groundnut field and uprooted several plants. As soon she realised what they were doing, she drove them out and collected the plants. She plucked the groundnuts, washed them and put them into her dhavani. He stepbrother came running, 'Are you plucking and eating groundnuts? I'll complain to Ayya.'

'Ey, the cows pulled them out.'

'Let's see,' he pulled at her dhavani and spilled the groundnuts. She tried to both stop him and pick the fallen groundnuts. In the confusion he ran and complained to their father who was engaged in a serious discussion.

'Aren't you an educated girl? Why do you always pick a quarrel with your brother? I was talking to someone when he called me, why did you hit him?'

'No, I didn't do anything to him.'

'Does that mean he is lying?'

Her stepmother had joined them by then. 'Because you are educated are we beneath you? Do you think you are a queen? Keep your education to yourself. Fucking education!' she screamed.

Startled by the suddenness of the incident and hurt by her stepmother's words, she shouted back, 'You whore!'

Before she could say anything more she tasted blood in her mouth. Her father had struck her.

Amma was out working in the field that day. When she returned home that evening, she advised her, 'You have come on your vacation. Keep your mouth tightly closed, like an oyster, and use words like they are pearls.'

'Look at her monkey face. What's the use of education? She has no respect for her elders and calls her stepmother a whore! How can she make good with her filthy mouth?' Her father cursed her as he ate his evening meal.

'Haughty, conceited and arrogant!' her stepmother joined in. 'She would have attacked me like a dog if you hadn't been there.'

Her face was swollen because she had been weeping. Amma remained silent. Perhaps she was following her own advice.

~

The next morning her mother left to attend a funeral in her native village. She had a bad cold and a splitting headache and was no longer talking to her stepmother. She made some tea for herself. Her brother had some of her tea. After drinking the tea, he applied coconut oil on his dry skin. Their stepmother walked past the kitchen.

Her father came home.

'There is no control whatsoever in this house. People make and drink tea on their own. In a large family, if everybody begins acting on their own, how do we manage the money? That fellow has emptied the bottle on his body, there isn't a drop of oil left. And he glares at me! Is there no one to question such behaviour? I am like a stone used to wipe shit, or maybe worse.' Her father could not bear such talk; he shouted at her and her brother.

When Amma returned, she tackled the situation. 'You can't bear the mere sight of my children, can you? She is here for her vacation, she is here for only two months in a year. Can't she make herself some tea when she has a headache? As for my son, he is toiling for this family in the hot sun, can't he apply some oil on his skin? And you complained to the man you garlanded and married in public.'

Her stepmother spent a lot of time provoking her mother. She would then complain to her husband and earn a round of blows for her mother.

TWELVE

The novelist, her mother and her siblings had lived as strangers in their own house. Envy, confusion and humiliation had oppressed their lives. But, was polygamy the cause of the oppressive atmosphere? The novelist believed that the peace, happiness and privacy of the family had been violated by the arrival of others.

Why do siblings quarrel with each other and sometimes even commit murder? Why do neighbours quarrel over trivial matters? Kathamuthu had offered protection to a vulnerable widow. Was that wrong of him? How had she become 'vulnerable'? What does being a 'widow' mean? What was the definition of 'protection'? Our values define these terms. Instead of viewing the unhappiness of her family against the background of societal and historical forces, the novelist simplistically blamed it on her father's polygamy. The author of the *Grip of Change* had misunderstood the concept of morality. Had she assessed her characters with value-based judgements, or with what she believed were personal experiences?

~

Her younger sister accompanied Sukumaran to show him the way to the field. But she came back home running, crying.

'The stranger, son of a bitch, said he did not know the way. So I sent this child to guide him.' Her mother snatched a broomstick and ran towards him, 'Did you grab her?' He fled for his life.

Lilly had smacked the slow-witted Gnanakoothan while helping him with maths. He had stolen her dhavani while she was bathing.

Suja's sister's husband came to see Suja in the hostel and requested her not to ever tell her sister that he had come. Suja was forced to live with the fear and guilt.

The novelist's life was full of encounters or narratives of such men. Or, she had remembered only those men when she wrote her novel.

~

The novelist's house faced the national highway. Rangam Pillai's house was on the other side of the highway. Manickam amma worked in his fields. A fearful story circulated that he had killed a lower caste boy, who had stolen some peanuts, by slapping him hard on his face. Having killed him, Rangam Pillai took the body to the well, cut off an ear and ate it. The novelist's mother had told her the story. No one knew why he had torn the boy's ear and eaten it. She was reminded of the saying 'The sin of killing will be rid in the eating.' He had probably believed that a killer would be forgiven if he ate the flesh of his victim. People also said that he steadily grew anaemic after that incident.

Manickam amma turned up dutifully every morning and slogged till late in the evening. Though Manickam amma was supposedly Pillai's concubine, the novelist had never seen her entering his house. If she had to go to the back yard of the house, she would take a roundabout route. As a child, the novelist had wondered how a woman could make love to a man who would not allow her to enter his house. Manickam amma's behaviour could be explained by certain facts—that she was a widow and that she had four or five children. Did that justify a sexual liaison? Perhaps the novelist might be able to answer the question.

~

'How long are you going to remain like this?'

'...'

'I think you've caught a cold. You might feel better if you get some fresh air.'

Amma touched her gently. 'Ayyo, you're burning. Why didn't you call me? Let me get you some warm water, you should take some medicine for your fever.'

The medicine made her drowsy.

~

The novelist spoke from within.

'Don't you know I am hyperactive when I have fever?'

'Can you remember what Kuldip told you?'

'Yes...What did she say? I can't really remember.'

~

Kuldip was wearing a red silk sari with a low cut blouse and drinking coffee when D.P. Singh started chatting with her. He engaged her in conversation and slowly manoeuvred her to a corner. She appeared delighted by the prospect.

'Come along for a stroll?'

She accepted his invitation. They walked for nearly four miles. They discussed forests, mountains, rivers, silkworm, noodles and sex. When they returned it was already eight in the evening. She nodded when he had said, 'Let's meet again same time tomorrow.'

Before she could slip into a world of new dreams, Yogesh interrupted her.

'Kuldip, did you go for a walk with that scoundrel?'

'Yes, are you jealous?'

'Nonsense, why I should feel jealous? Do you know what he has been saying about you?'

Kuldip was shocked into silence.

'He made a bet that he would go out with you. I was there when it happened.'

'Then?'

'Then? He says he has booked a room in Hotel Anjana. He is certain that he will have you. He also says that he would be benevolent to you! Do you have to sink that low? He set up the challenge to insult us!'

~

The novelist continued.

'Wasn't Kuldip hurt? She did not believe Yogesh at first and confirmed the story through a couple of other sources. The next day, when D.P. called her, she refused to go with him. Thereafter, D.P. leered at her whenever he saw her, "Super rhythm... super rhythm!" Don't you remember? Do you remember anything at all these days?'

'So the rural Manickam amma and the urban Kuldip contributed to your story. Of course, combined with other incidents you have heard about. A story that could explain the nature of the lower caste Thangam's relationship with the upper caste Udayar. How did the telling of such a story interest you?'

Movies show lovers transcending caste, religion and class. They find solace in death and earn their place in eternity. What is the basis of such stories? How did the novelist venture to write a story that questioned the purity of love, especially in the prevailing atmosphere of belief in it?

She was almost asleep...

They had excised themselves from the tumour that was society. A silver cascade formed their backdrop. It was noteworthy that the extras in the frame were wearing white. The ideal lovers – freed from caste, creed, religion, etc – were singing and dancing on the flower-filled mountainside, as a woman and a man. The music was pleasant.

The awareness, that the dream would end shortly, persisted.

THIRTEEN

Her fever subsided, but the fatigue remained. She felt that nothing had meaning or value. A sense of nihilism swept over her. What good would it do to review a work bearing the weight and pressure of her present life? There could never be any certainty, her personal and public lives would be constantly impinged by change. She kept swinging between states of confusion and clarity.

Chinnukannu Annan, a panchayat union employee, had come to visit her. He always quoted the famous lines when he met her, ever since her childhood, 'Instead of nurturing Sivakami, we should nurture a plaintain tree. It would at least yield fruit.' That day she agreed with the truth of his words.

'Are you feeling unwell?'

'Yes, Anna,' her voice wobbled. She had always addressed him as elder brother.

He sensed her unhappiness, 'Is something wrong at home?'

'No, Anna.'

There was a smile on his dark face that drew an answering smile from her. She wondered at the sense of ease that could be found in relationships not based on bargains and commitments.

But the relationship between Chinnakannu and the novelist's father had been different. He had once worked as an agricultural labourer for her father. His contract at that time required him to show up at eight in the morning and begin the day's work without waiting for anyone's orders. He would get his share of the produce immediately after the harvest. Her father would be furious when Chinnakannu came late. Chinnakannu would sometimes complain about the extra work. As a child she had adored Chinnakannu, her father had been the villain in her eyes.

She had resolved not to become her father. Was it possible to live without commitments, contracts or expectations? The novel's heroine Gowri had hated her father. Because he had married many women and made her childhood unnatural and miserable. His words and actions had hardly matched. As a politician he had always worked towards acquiring power. He had tyrannically dominated the people around him. Gowri of the novel had been a young, impressionable girl with no experience of the world outside her home. Her perspective had not been tempered by life experience. So she had wished to be the antithesis of Kathamuthu.

Did creativity begin with a difference of opinion?

✵

She went to her friend's house for coffee. The talk turned sickeningly, once again, to the disease-ridden literary world. She began to enquire about their daughters with interest, forcing the conversation to take a new turn.

'The little one has written a story,' their father, her friend, announced.

'Really, what's it about?'

'The father of the family brings home a rose plant, and everyone in the family is glad,' the girl told her. 'But the father is always busy and the mother falls sick. The rose plant dies.'

'Why did you choose that subject?' The novelist wanted to know.

'My father is always busy and doesn't spend time at home...' The father and mother smiled at each other. There were a few moments of uncomfortable silence following the girl's direct statement.

She said to herself, 'We can keep the spirit of creativity alive in ourselves only if we refuse to become our fathers.'

✵

Her novel had died. The novelist had also died. Once the antithesis had become the thesis, the words transformed into soundless wind.

One must water the plant continuously expecting roses! Who has the patience? Why should anyone need roses?

She heard many voices, but she could not comprehend the opinions they were expressing. Neither could she continue her journey onward. Fatigue gripped her.

~

The novelist had struggled to complete her novel. She had only wanted to portray the deep roots of caste oppression in villages, and how violence erupted even within a caste group. She had, in fact, ended her novel with Thangam becoming Kathamuthu's third wife. She had marked the full stop. But her pen was compelled to go further.

As the story proceeded, the core disappeared in the details of Kathamuthu's characterisation. There were suggestions that the core issue must be kept free from such narrative compulsions. She was told that socialist realism was not merely the reflection of society, and that a logical analysis should be presented, connecting the past with the present and the future. She was advised that the author's intention ought to be revealed in full clarity to the reader.

The novelist had erased the full stop and continued. The character Nallasivam emerged, narrating his own story. The novelist was just a mute witness. Chandran who began to work in the rice mill was like many other workers of the novelist's acquaintance. But in the story, Chandran organised the workers in order to keep the mentor of the novel happy. The pen was amazing, it had extended the story, overriding the novelist's conclusion.

FOURTEEN

The novelist wished for a change in the leadership of the scheduled castes. She wished for a revolutionary leadership. It was just simple arithmetic according to her—two plus two is four. Nallasivam, like Kathamuthu, is a self-centered Vanniyar leader. Both fall on the wayside of progress. In the novel, the Dalits and the Vanniyars accepted the leadership of Chandran.

Easy! The Vanniars are poor and the Dalits are poor; what if they join together in a powerful movement! Nothing but arithmetic. The novel presents a logical solution!

When she ended the novel with Thangam becoming the third wife of Kathamuthu, she wanted to be sure that her words provided satisfactory expression to her intent, and gave the manuscript to a literary friend. His comment was, 'It is not good to expose a Dalit leader's exploitation of his own community. A leader who is conscious of his Dalit identity will not be exploitative, or rather should not be. Even if he is exploitative, exposing him will only strengthen the opposition. Therefore, create an honest youth within the community and allow him to play the role of a revolutionary. Similarly, find a man among the Vanniars.'

The novelist's friend believed that if writers, novelists, maths teachers and intellectuals scribbled on paper that Vanniyars and Dalits must unite, that it might really happen. He said, 'We must at least express our desire for such an union.'

The novelist, carried away by his suggestions, added a tail to her novel and gave it to him again for a reading. He felt that the end portion had not shaped up well. That was her first novel. Writing, correcting, rewriting, seeking opinions and carrying out corrections had consumed a considerable amount of time. She could not wait to be rid of it. After she sent the final draft, the manuscript remained asleep for a year at Annam Publications.

In the villages of northern districts, atrocities were committed on Dalits by the Backward Castes who had absorbed Brahminism. When the novel was written, a number of violent clashes were taking place between Vanniars and Parayars. People were attacked, tortured and killed. The novelist suggested inter-caste marriage and a united struggle against casteism when she was asked, 'Amma, what solution can you offer?'

Instead of writing that Dalits should organise themselves around the focal point of Dalit identity, fight against oppression and extract equality by presenting a united front, she had suggested that Dalits join hands with those who perpetrated violence on them—the Vanniyars. It is impossible to ignore the novelist as a rope and at the same time she cannot be killed as a snake!

~

A decade has passed since the completion of the novel. It was a good opportunity to check whether the contents of the novel and contemporary reality match. Was there a Chandran in the making? Are there many Gowris in the pattern of the unmarried Gowri in the novel? Nallasivam—has he died? Has there been a change in the Vanniyar leadership?

She had met her literary friend recently and he had asked her, 'Things have been happening according to the predictions in your novel, haven't they?' The question disgusted the novelist. How can a man be satisfied by such false assumptions? He now saw himself as a prophet! Dalits are gaining strength and threatening to become a powerful force. And there are people who believe that unity between castes is possible by the coming together of powerful and self-centered individuals!

The novelist projected herself as a responsible person by offering a solution to a social problem. There are many like her who write formulaic stories. Poor and helpless villagers are exploited by a rich landlord, the sole representative of power in the village. Revolutionary intellectuals with their typical jute bags enter the villages, conduct night school, create awareness and raise consciousness among the villagers. The villagers in turn stand united, irrespective of caste and creed, and fight oppression. Thus end the stories. A sprinkling of female characters are added to spice the preparation.

What is the novelist's perception of life?

Has she travelled the same old path or has she found a new track?

Here, class and caste are almost the same. The lower castes are also the have-nots, and the haves are the upper castes; the division is clear. They cannot avoid clashing with each other. As the lower castes are several and divided, they are not able to offer a tough fight to the upper castes. The lower castes should shatter their particular identities and identify themselves as one class. The Dalits form the last rung of the labour class. If the struggle is centred on the Dalits, class and caste equality will be attained.

It appears that the novelist unquestioningly accepted the above interpretation of class and caste. She constructed events in her narrative to suit this interpretation. The older generation is casteist. Therefore, in her story, she removed those characters and created fresh characters to fit her theory. She has not adequately explained the commonalities and differences between caste and class. She went ahead merging them at her own sweet convenience! In order to hide such inadequacies, she cleverly fluffed the story with descriptions of real-life rural activities such as the village market and the preparation of pork on a festival day.

Can life and writing be possible without generalisation? If there was no generalised perception of life, how would novels be written?

Why had the novelist not even thought of raising such questions? Had she been intoxicated by her own views? If rejection or acceptance is based on need, what was the novelist's need to accept those views?

FIFTEEN

In the novel, the *Grip of Change*, the pigs ran about energetically. There were no descriptions of their body hair drying into sharp needles after a mud bath; of the mother pig lying on its flabby stomach with piglets competing to find a nipple; of people not being allowed to defecate in peace because the pigs would butt them away with their hungry mouths. The novelist had not described the filthiness of the pigs. She had only described the people who ate their meat. Jesus Christ had driven the demons out of a man's body and had commanded them to enter into the bodies of pigs. The maddened pigs had then drowned themselves! George Orwell had created some communist pigs in his *Animal Farm*. In Tolstoy's story "Yardstick", the horses fall in love like humans. There are a number of stories describing dogs and their gratitude. The crow teaches us unity. When two birds fly in the sky, a number of poets are inspired to write poems on love.

If one has to write about pigs, one has to be prepared to taste shit as they do. She smiled. When she attempted to list the memories kindled by the thought of pigs, she felt as though she was testing the limits of the human brain.

What kind of a person is the novelist? How is she represented in the novel? What has she attempted to comprehend through literature and what has she actually understood?

Does the novel reflect her desire to seek answers for the numerous questions generated by life? Or does it reflect an arrogance that constricts life within her narrow understanding and limited knowledge? Does her work have literary merit?

The novelist had attempted to visualise the novel in its most complete form. Kathamuthu had been the beginning. Of a rare breed, he was articulate, ambitious and talented. He utilised his talents to forge a career for himself. With time his activities became self-serving, and his creative energy was eroded by capitulation to pleasurable indulgences. And his upper caste associates had encouraged the degeneration. The story ended with the replacement of Kathamuthu by less self-centered individuals. When many writers presented sexual perversions as factors responsible for caste oppression, her novel had painted caste in all its dimensions. The oppression of women had been interwoven with the problems of caste. Thus, in order to claim a completeness of vision, the novelist had deviated from social realities and attempted to perceive life according to her convenience. After the revolution everyone lived happily ever after—to seek such a form of completion appears childish.

In the space between the sky and the earth, characterised by loneliness, the chirping of the birds causes exultation. Amidst the crowded street in sultry weather, a piece of cool clear sky causes elation. Close observation of society too inspires people. The novelist-author had paid attention to Kannamma, Kathamuthu, Gowri…She had stolen Kathamuthu's satire and exhibited it as her own.

～

'May I know why you laughed?'

The novelist laughed some more without replying.

'When your father ordered you to write a petition, you changed a few words and felt triumphant about it. But don't you realise that society existed as he had summed it up? I pity you!'

Laughter.

'Kathamuthu had enjoyed setting his wives against each other. Whereas you had united them and had greater fun!

'Kathamuthu had ridiculed Thangam's name and baited her for not knowing her father's name. And you had mocked Kathamuthu by marrying Thangam to him finally.

'Kannamma was not spared. You could not help laughing at everything she did—whether she walked, talked or stood. Old age and lack of education are matters to be laughed at. Won't you become old, or lose your sight, or die, for that matter?

'Then the sub-collector's visit! The sub-collector distributes relief to those whose huts were burned in the fire. He distributes saris and veshtis. One of the women who went to receive the sari impatiently grabs it from his hand without waiting for the photograph to be taken. You placed yourself in the position of the sub-collector and had a hearty laugh!

'You enjoyed describing the Paraya boy at the Udayar's house. His hunger and his victimhood made you laugh hysterically.

'You address the rapist Udayar, the tahsildar, the police and other upper caste men respectfully in first person plural. Whereas the rest do not even appear to be human beings in your eyes!'

~

The novelist had been studying in college. Ramasamy, who had been in school with her, was herding cattle. They had met on the road accidentally.

'Ramasamy, how are you da?'

He retaliated, 'What do you mean "da"?'

Silence.

SIXTEEN

She had travelled quite a distance from the novelist. She saw herself differing from the hopeful and egoistic novelist. She felt alienated from the novel, the *Grip of Change*.

The novelist's father knew that he and Kathamuthu were not the same person. However, he was a significant presence in the novelist's life, so he tried to compare himself with Kathamuthu. He found the characterisation cruel and damaging, and was saddened by it. He thought that the novelist had taken revenge on him.

Her father, mother and stepmother came to Allahabad. Her father was proud of her. Indira Gandhi was campaigning in the Amethi constituency for her son Rajiv. 'I gave my younger son to the service of this nation. Unfortunately God has taken him away. Now, I dedicate my elder son...' People applauded the speech. While she admired a person's capacity to make such a speech, her father felt happy about his daughter's physical proximity to Indira Gandhi. However, on the day the votes were being counted, she came home at one in the morning. Her father opened the door, looked at the clock and went back to sleep without a word.

Her father was in a good mood when he bathed in Prayag and was taken around in a horse cart. He expressed his desire to leave the world and proceed to the forest like the sages of yore. On seeing a homeless man on the road wearing a thick coat of dirt and examining his genitalia, her father had been shocked. Throughout the journey he made happy conversation with his wives.

He walked fast on the dirty roads of Kasi. When they approached a Brahmin to perform the rites for the forefathers, he had enquired about their kulam, gothram and other details of caste. The Brahmin had expressed his appreciation of her, 'You will benefit from this virtuous deed. You have brought your parents to Kasi and enabled them to bathe in the Ganga.'

Her father quickly retorted, 'She has not brought us here, I brought these three here.'

The Brahmin persisted, 'You have come to Kasi because she lives in Allahabad. So she is responsible for bringing you here.'

Her father was amused by the argument. Finally, everything depended on the lord of Kasi, Visweswaran.

As the train tickets had not been reserved in advance, her parents had to stand on their journey back to Madras. Though she bought her father many things that he liked, and treated her mother and her stepmother with equal respect, he did not trust her. He felt that he was always being scrutinised. At times he felt unwanted. How difficult it is to be an object of observation! How could he be cordial to her when she constantly watched him with suspicion. She realised the extent to which she had affected him only when she went home for a visit.

He was bed-ridden, sick, with a long beard and mustache. She was studying her father even as he was in distress. She felt tears pricking her eyes as she stood near him to enquire about his health.

'Because he stood all through the journey his feet became swollen. He has been ill since then.'

'My health has been affected because of her. When she joined duty, I offered to accompany her. She ignored my offer and told me to stay at home. She also said that people would misunderstand her. I felt insulted because I had educated her. When parents struggle hard to educate their children, the children are only worried about their image. How many such educated brats have I come across? Many of them have risen from their seats to salute me! This woman asked me not to go with her! Because she is educated—her education is not worth even a single pubic hair! If she could tell that to someone like me, what would have happened if I had been just a plain farmer? I would have been forced to wash her feet and drink that water. Get lost. Don't show your face till I'm a corpse. You think that you are an officer. But there will come a time when I will be on a parliamentary committee asking you questions. You'll have to lower your head in shame.'

She stood there, crying. She could not fit in completely in the world of her work. She could not wholly extricate herself from her family. She stood there beside her father not knowing where to proceed. Her brothers and sisters had aligned themselves with their father. They were not kind to her either. Though she stood in isolation, there was a peculiar pride informing her posture.

'You did not even send a peon or a vehicle to buy the tickets... What's the point of all this? Just leave.'

She left the room and lay down in her usual corner. She wanted to be left alone. But her brother's children peeped and left.

'Athai is weeping! Athai is weeping!'

After a while, her stepmother entered the room. 'I am not lying. He kept lamenting that you did not respect him. The train was very crowded. There was no place even to stand. The journey lasted two days, so his legs became swollen. Why are you crying?

He is pleased that you came to see him. Though he appears harsh, he loves his children.'

Her sisters questioned her, 'We have never seen Ayya like this. He was so upset, he kept repeating "She refused to take me with her when she joined duty." Why did you behave like that?'

'You should not have hurt him, he was so proud of you.'

Her mother was the last to come. 'Look, your eyes are swollen with all this weeping. You believe everything the old man says and cry! The money he had borrowed was all over. If he had told you when he wanted to leave for Madras you could have booked the tickets. In fact, you asked him as soon as we reached Allahabad. His response was that you were keen to get rid of us! How is it possible to get tickets with just two days notice? You did try to get tickets even then by sending a person to the station. Anyway, was he the only one who travelled standing? A number of people were standing on that train! In the train, he picked up a quarrel. And he caught a cold due to the change in climate and water. What can you do about that? Don't cry! Even when he is sick, if Periyayi comes – hahaha – they will talk and laugh. He is a fraud. If you hand over your salary and request money from him for your day-to-day expenses, he will say there is no one like my daughter!'

'But Amma…' she mentioned her sisters' comments.

'Tell me, has your father gone to anybody's house and wet his hands? Did your sisters feed him for a single day? You had bought so many things expecting his arrival. I don't even know what they are called. You are a grown woman crying because of what people say! Why did you study so much? In order to cry and be laughed at? Get up and drink some tea.'

SEVENTEEN

The novelist was in the SFI movement for a short while. At Padi, during the workers' agitation under the leadership of V.P. Chinthan she had walked in a procession with Parvathi Menon and Vani, shouting slogans. She attended a meeting where Athreya presented a critical analysis of the budget from the point of view of the poor. She did not jot down points. But she took note of the fair-skinned woman with him. Later her association with SFI came to an end with her maiden speech – The role of women in creating a new India – at a north Madras slum.

During holidays, in order to avoid the bitterness, the rivalry, the confusion and the crowd at home, she would take the cattle out for grazing. She would clear the thorn shrubs and lie down on the bare earth to entertain desultory thoughts. She attended an interview for a job at the Archives. She, in fact, received the appointment letter asking her to report within a week's time.

Parvati Menon advised her to concentrate on the Archives and forget about appearing for the civil services examination. She said that working for the Indian Administrative Service would be like working as a head clerk in a firm. Working at the Archives would give her time to work for the movement. Since her father was particular that she should take up a career with the IAS, and because she had already written the exam, she had to think before taking up Parvati's advice. She vaguely remembered that Parvathi's father too had taken the exam and had been absorbed into the Indian Foreign Service. He was posted in an Indian embassy in some foreign country.

Parvathi's opinion and similar views expressed by other people had considerably reduced the importance of the IAS for her. She no longer perceived it as enormously prestigious. Moreover, her father knew neither Hindi nor English. It had seemed unnecessary to take him along when she went to take up her first posting. When she examined her motives and feelings she could not find any of the faults that her father had attributed to her. She accepted her mother's explanation; her mother knew her father better than she did.

Except her mother, it seemed to her that every other person in the family had moved away from her. There was a possibility that her mother would also join them as she too was under constant surveillance. What separated all of them from her? If education could damage human relations to such an extent, was it then necessary to be educated? Why was every person turning out to be a culprit? She suspected that institutionalised education of the unquestioning kind and her mother's influence ruled high in her novel.

∾

She was walking on a varappu. On the wet clay earth, kuvalai flowers were in full bloom. A buffalo made its way ahead devastating the flowers. While kuvalai and rose are both flowers, why are they referred to differently—'kuvalai malar' and 'roja poo'? Both malar and poo mean flower. Because kuvalai was introduced through Sangam poetry we refer to it as a malar, whereas the rose blooms in every garden, therefore it is called roja poo. When language is the expression of one's own experience, what then is Dalit language, or the language of the oppressed?

Is it just writing about huge pits full of shit and pigs roaming in the neighbourhood of such pits, ignoring traditional descriptions about the moon and the stars in the sky, and the colourful kolam decorating the front yard every dawn? Or replacing the names Ranganatha Iyer and Vasakam Pillai with Kathamuthu, Chinnan, Chengandi, etc? Or replacing rice, paruppu and ghee with red cholam and sour keerai? Or replacing words like idiot with sister-fucker?

What is the language of the novelist? Has she written mechanically to suit her cooked-up story or is there life in her language? Has she lived with those characters and what has been her experience? She would have to clarify this personally.

∾

She appeared, with short hair, wearing a parrot-green silk sari with zari border.

'You have accused me with regard to human relations, haven't you?'

'Yes, where are you from?'

'Perambalur, earlier in Trichy District, now in Thiruvalluvar District.'

'Kulam, gotram, caste?'

'All three are the same—Parayar.'

'Without branching into philosophical digressions, please provide a brief account of your life.'

'My father's name is Palanimuthu; my mother's name is Thandayi. My stepmother's name is Chellammal. We were thirteen children besides two who were adopted. Adding the two grandmothers, twenty of us lived in one house. We owned small plots of irrigated as well as dry land. My father spent his childhood collecting pig shit. Thanks to the backbreaking labour of my grandparents, my father and his siblings, we came to own some land.

'When I was born, my father had already completed his tenure as an MLA. I have not been able to locate details regarding his political career. I do not know which political party he belonged to. I can clearly remember that immediately after the inoculation against small pox I had gone to play in the paddy field where my father was plowing the land. As a result I fell ill. Our house had been constructed by selling some of our land in addition to the loan that my father had obtained from his elder brother. After my father died, when I scanned his diaries from 1952 to 1957—I learnt that nothing worthwhile had been discussed in the assembly and that no one cared about the welfare of Dalits. There were also laundry and MLA mess accounts in his diaries. He often said that he would even stoop to the extent of begging in order to educate his children. He hated us wearing flowers or jewellery of any kind.'

'Please be brief.'

'Though occasionally we were victims of poverty, the elders shared all the burden and responsibility. We were to be mostly found working in the fields except during school hours. Don't you know, we grew up in difficult circumstances?'

'So you used familiar life with not so familiar imagination and tried to tell a story in a traditional narrative form?'

'Yes.'

'You changed zila to district and taluka to circle, and felt proud about the changes. What does the episode convey? That you hold spoken language inferior to written language? You used peoples' language within quotes and attempted to decorate their language with your narration. You saw yourself as different from them and therefore you could not portray their life or the aesthetics of their life effectively. You did not comprehend that their life *is* literature; therefore, your expression was limited by existing literary standards.'

'Do you mean to deny that writing as a form constructs its own language?'

'There were many who attempt to enslave us through their writings. They call our spoken language 'slum language' and deride it. Without providing special consideration for written language, language should be constructed on the basis of life experience and the questioning of life. We do not need to take refuge in replacing the nine-yard madisar with the loin cloth, performing a mechanical translation in the name of skill or identity...'

'Dear critic, enough, did you have to focus on me, of all people? Why do you play with me, making one half known and the other, unknown?'

'Why do I do it? You silly...because you were proud that your novel had been widely discussed...self-examination...'

APPENDIX

TWO READINGS

AND ONE SHALL LIVE IN TWO...

Nineteen eighty-nine is by far the most important and defining year in the history of the Dalit movement in Tamil Nadu: the Bodi riots in Tirunelveli that claimed a dozen lives marked the upsurge of the Pallars under the leadership of John Pandian, Irumborai Gunasekaran and Vadivel Ravanan (as well as their consequent incarceration by the government); the agitations against Vanniyar atrocities in northern Tamil Nadu by the Dalit umbrella organisation Scheduled Caste Liberation Movement (SCALM) with leaders like L. Ilayaperumal Sakthidasan and Vai. Balasundaram; the parliamentary elections that saw the break-up of SCALM due to petty electoral politics; and the Dalit Panthers' pulsating slogans and protest rallies that rattled the state machinery in Madurai under the new-found leadership of Thirumaavalavan. It was in such an awakened yet tense atmosphere that Sivakami's *Pazhaiyana Kazhithalum* was published to critical acclaim and popular appeal.

The first Tamil novel by a Dalit woman, it evoked a great deal of discussion because it went beyond condemning caste fanatics by using fiction to describe how we were shackled, and tangled among ourselves. Instead of being the journey of her individual voice and consciousness, it was a unanimous expression of the youth of this oppressed community—eager and waiting for change.

~

In the *Grip of Change*, a novel of critical realism, Gowri views her father Kathamuthu, the local Dalit leader, with an attitude of contempt. By speaking of his tyrannical overbearingness, corruption and polygamy, Sivakami has reflected the universal trend that powerful men usually lead pathetic personal lives. Here, the acute portrayal of Kathamuthu and the women in his life, captures the unseen, unedited side of Dalit patriarchy. The significance of the book lies in the fact that it speaks for the most vulnerable members of the Dalit community—its women.

The rare beauty and honesty of the narrative arises from its body-centricity. Thangam's body bears testimony to the difficulties faced by Dalit women. On a closer reading, it looks like a major, defining part of the novel was entirely played out on the Dalit woman Thangam's body. Her battered body frames the opening scene; her history is constituted by her widowhood (hence she becomes a 'surplus' woman), the harassment by her brothers-in-law when she refuses to submit to them, the sexploitation by her caste Hindu landlord, the assault on her by caste Hindu men (owing to sexual/social 'misdemeanour'), and so on. Even her struggle for land is linked to her body and her fertility—she does not have children, and so her brothers-in-law refuse to give her a share in the family land. When she is sheltered and fed by Kathamuthu, her vulnerability is exploited; she is forced to physically yield to his desires. The same body, through which she was oppressed and subjugated, also grants her the power to gain ascendancy in Kathamuthu's house and gives her dominance over his wives.

The narrative and the turn of events are at once authentic and terrifying. A single woman's life is capable of sparking a caste riot. Her casual existence, marked by mute submission and stubborn resistance at varying points of time, can trigger so many events that will leave several lives forever changed.

In negotiating and trying to probe into inter-caste sexual relations, the author sheds light on how patriarchy gets diluted on its way down the caste ladder. In the affair between the Dalit

Kathamuthu and the caste Hindu widow Nagamani, she earns a rightful place by being 'installed' as his wife in his home. Conversely, Paranjothi Udayar who forces himself on Thangam, at best engages her as a mistress. She is not brought within the confines of a socially acknowledged/approved relationship because of her outcasteness. Then, caste purity is not protected only through control of caste Hindu women, but also through the absence of social sanction to certain inter-caste relationships.

How do women react to such circumstances where caste and convention (morality) are sidestepped? The Dalit woman Kanagavalli, Kathamuthu's first wife, remains a mute spectator and even develops a bonding of friendship with his second wife Nagamani. On the other hand, Kamalam, wife of Paranjothi Udayar, incites her brothers to assault her husband's mistress Thangam. And the climax lies in Thangam 'earning' a place in Kathamuthu's home. Because caste seemingly does not have a role in this, patriarchy poses in loneliness for the snapshots and Kathamuthu resembles a vicious womaniser.

It is to her credit that Sivakami does not glamourise sexuality by sprinkling the book with careless elopements and clumsy marriages. Instead, every relationship is played out to a striking finale. Not only with regard to the main characters, but also the minor ones. She speaks to us of caste that appears even in the silence of shattered love with the episode of Lalitha and Elangovan. Likewise, she dismantles the widespread caste Hindu assumption/notion that love/sex among the Dalit castes is unrestricted, by showing the slow progress and social taboos that regulate the relationship of the Dalit lovers Sargunam and Rasendran.

Sivakami criticises the Dalit movement and exposes the cruel face of Dalit patriarchy through feminist eyes, and yet, clearly veers away from becoming a 'caste traitor' because of her engagement with the search for solutions.

In a world where navel-gazing masquerades as a profession, such deep portrayals of the dynamics of caste and sexuality deserve our applause.

~

Sivakami is a shrewd mistress of her art. Eight years after the publication of her first novel, she revisited it and provided the *Author's Notes* that would surpass any critic's probe, in its excruciating dissection of subjectivities where she herself is not spared.

And by self-translating both these works, Sivakami has once again entered the realm of re-rendering and re-interpretation, and has completed yet another re-visitation.

'Nothing in the novel was untrue. But the novel was false, she felt.' How many writers would ever have the courage to write thus of their first novel? Not unless they decide to dethrone their egos and attempt critical self-examination. How often does this happen?

But *Author's Notes* is really neither about Kathamuthu nor Gowri, nor the author, but about the maturity and perspective that comes with the passage of time. It is about the change that is happening, the past that has faded away, it is about the present trying to dream its future.

In the dense second novel, Sivakami raises all our questions. By taking on both roles – of the critic and the author – has she conveniently appropriated for herself even the avenues for criticism? Or does the author aim to mock at readers, telling them that fiction is more than fiction, that a certain politics has pervaded her writing?

By writing this, not only did she distance herself from the first book, but preempted critical probing with her intense self-examination. *Author's Notes* declares, 'I have the questions, and the answers.' And if we have more questions about Gowri's story, whom should we address them to? For instance, when Gowri refuses to marry, is it because she is a victim of her mother's experience? Or is it a brave assertion that she is walking away from the victimhood of her mother? Or is it merely independence?

Gowri detests her father's two qualities—his polygamy and his coarseness. The antitheses, monogamy and refinement, are the basic signs of human evolution into 'civilisation'. Does her emancipatory modernity then seek to 'civilise' Kathamuthu? In doing so, what exactly are her prejudices? What role does primitivism have to play in a father–daughter relationship? On the other hand, hasn't modernity always been an issue taken up only by the 'upper' caste woman?

When the margin is the centre, every word becomes an arena for contestation. Sivakami's strength lies in the fact that she does not seek to convince. She merely moves on.

~

Sivakami devotes her strongest prose to the depiction of the relationship between Kathamuthu and Gowri. Despite all their differences – which the novel painstakingly points out – in the end, they serve the same people and they (prepare to) fight the same enemies. There is much in common between them—the thesis and the antithesis. Kathamuthu might dislike communism and treat it as a new-fangled idea, and Gowri may abhor her father's innate manipulativeness and his weaknesses. Their separate ways have distinctive drawbacks. Yet, both of them envision an end to the atrocities against Dalits. Not only are they of one blood, but they also share the same living dream. Literature has reclaimed that lifeline and that dream. And thus, one shall live in two.

Meena Kandasamy
Chennai
November 2005

Meena Kandasamy is an independent writer based in Chennai. She has translated the writings and speeches of Viduthalai Chiruthaigal leader, Thol. Thirumaavalavan.

ONCE UPON A TIME THERE WAS A NOVEL

Sivakami writes a novel and attaches a sequel that takes up the painful task of deconstructing the novel. Painful, because it is difficult to trample upon what one has created. It is agonising to perform a dance of destruction stamping on what one has undertaken to create. Sivakami dares to do it with some strange results in terms of both writing a novel and making it a text to be read.

After reading both the novel and the sequel deconstructing the novel, the intelligent and intellectual reader would want to go back to the novel and differentiate the various aspects and hang them separately, and observe them and examine them for any defects. The reader may want to know what went into the making of Thangam or Kathamuthu or Gowri. But I did not attempt to revisit the novel. Normally, I am the kind of reader who lets a piece of writing to flow all over me, allowing me to experience its undercurrents and its whirlpools. Sometimes I float along and sometimes I stumble on slippery stones; and sometimes, I collect beautiful stones shaped by the flow. I enjoy and question as I go along. The slow erosion of Kathamuthu's power, Gowri as the watchful observer, the women of the household allowing a third person to become part of it and the ensuing dialogues and conflicts, the manipulation of people's lives while political power is being built and destroyed, caste as a thread running through all of this—I could see the dexterity with which the author guides us through the narrative, elaborating all these details. Atrocities which one has learnt to accept as a part of daily routine – like the Panchayat school turning into an exclusive school for Parayars, the drama of compensation for burned houses, the exploitation of agricultural labourers and the power of the upper caste over the bodies of women of lower caste – unfold like a drama in constant mode of sarcastic underplay by the actors concerned. There are arguments, fights, manipulations, violence and tears; but strangely, they don't come out as being over-dramatised or over-emphasised. All this is part of what we call Indian life—to be lived, assessed, understood and tackled by us. And amidst all this, there is space for love, affection, food preparation and festivals. Sivakami paints minute details on a huge canvas, colouring some parts of it dark and drawing other parts with subtle lines merely indicating a few details, leaving it to the imagination of the readers to follow those lines for a fuller picture. I had some questions as well: Why does sexual power work differently for women and men of different castes? Why is it that the lower caste woman is raped by the upper caste man, but the lower caste man always sexually satiates the upper caste woman? Is Gowri the child Sivakami? And so on. Not that I wanted immediate answers.

~

After the novel, the sequel initially came as an assault and then it seemed like a clever attempt at preempting criticism. And then it became something else.

The act of writing is always accompanied by doubts, hesitation, despair and anguish. In the process of writing itself there is embellishment, exaggeration and selection. One is constantly holding back certain things and allowing some other elements to gain priority. Writing is not about truth but about experiencing a certain truth in many different ways. Writing cannot reflect reality but it can enhance, diminish and obliterate reality. Sivakami's sequel to the novel is about this process of writing, about choosing some and leaving out others, about deep-lying hatred that can alter truth, and about life experiences that change perspectives. By itself, the novel would have been just a novel about how caste permeates our life and how current politics play upon it. The sequel gives it further dimensions, adding some elements and taking away some. The sequel almost tries to take over the novel, but stops short, giving the novel its own space. What looks like an attempt at self-flagellation, when one begins to read the sequel, slowly turns into another act of creation.

So we have two creations reminiscent of the before and after images that come with some health treatments, although the images here are in the reverse. First is the novel with its entire expanse touching upon facts and experiences that belong to contemporary caste-based politics and life, unsparing in its treatment of people, events and happenings. Then comes the sequel with the novel wounded and scarred. The attempt is to create a text and then proceed to destroy it entirely with mockery, accusation and self-reflection. The text is then laid out on the table with all its hidden aspects revealed and then we suddenly realise that the text is not really dead, but now has added meanings—different entries and different exits. The text has metamorphosed into another text.

They say a ritual is sometimes performed in Benares. When a child is born after the loss of many children, the child is brought to Benares and the parents take the child with the priests in a boat to the middle of the river Ganga and pretend to throw the child into the water. The child is dipped in the water and taken out immediately. The mock ritual is performed to deceive fate. Thinking the child is dead, fate leaves it alone. Other such attempts are also made to hoodwink fate. A child is thrown on garbage as if it is not needed, and fate is deceived. Sometimes they also give the child derogatory names like Kuppai or Puzhudhi, as if the child was just garbage or dust, pretending that it is unloved and unwanted. And fate turns aside. Sivakami's novel, followed by the attempt to deconstruct the novel, reminds me of such mock attempts. After writing the novel, Sivakami denudes the novel and lays it bare. She dismembers it, makes deep gashes on its body, deep enough to reveal the bones. Not satisfied, she takes out some bones and rattles them. It is a novel that comes attached with a suicide note. Fortunately for the readers, although the suicide note is well written, the rope is not long enough.

C.S. Lakshmi
Mumbai
November 2005

C.S. Lakshmi is an independent researcher and writer. She writes in Tamil under the pseudonym Ambai. She is the founder-trustee and director of SPARROW (Sound and Picture Archives for Research on Women).

SELECT GLOSSARY

Aavani	The fifth month in the Tamil calendar, mid August–mid September
Araignan	A thick thread worn on the waist, used to tie the loin cloth. For toddlers, it is made of silver.
Arappu	Herbal powder used to wash hair
Ayudha poojai	A Hindu festival in which the tools and implements used by farmers, artisans and others are worshipped
Cheri	A village within a village where the Scheduled castes live, something like a ghetto
Chittirai	The first month in the Tamil calendar, mid April–mid May
Dhavani	Also known as half-sari, an upper garment worn over a long skirt, by young girls
Dinamani	Tamil newspaper
Dinathandi	Tamil newspaper
Gothram	Gothrams refer to the tribal clans of Rig Vedic pastural society. Marriage within the same gothram is prohibited.
Javvadu	A herbal perfume with a strong, sweet smell
Jhimki	Bell-shaped earring
Kanakambaram	Odourless flower, commonly found in pinkish red and orange colours
Kuladeivam	Family deity. Dalits in villages normally worship them as their ancestors.
Kulam	Pond

Kungumam	A bright red mark, normally worn on the forehead by women
Kunjam	A hair ornament worn at the end of a plait
Kulavai	The ululation made by women on suspicious occasions
Malar	Flower (formal usage)
Mandapam	A huge hall, used for marriages, meetings, etc
Mantram	Chanting of choice words to invoke the gods
Marudhani	Paste of marudhani leaves, when applied on hands and feet, stains red (Henna)
Marukkozhundu	A fragrant green herb, used along with other colourful and fragrant flowers to make a garland
Minor chain	A gold chain usually worn by landlords in rural areas
Mohini pisasu	A demon in the form of a beautiful and seductive woman
Molam	Drum
Namaskaram	Gesture of respect, expressed by folding hands, and more formally, by prostrating
Para-molam	The drum used by Parayars
Pillaiyar	The Hindu god with an elephant head
Pongal	A Tamil harvest festival celebrated in January
Poo	Flower (colloquial usage)
Pottu	A dot-shaped mark made on the forehead
Punnakku	The remains of oil seeds after the oil has been extracted
Punugu	Perfume prepared from the secretion of a civet cat
Samandi	Yellow- or orange-coloured flowers
Samadhi	Graveyard

Siakkai	Herbal powder used to cleanse hair
Sirumullai	A fragrant flower of the jasmine family with small, needle-like petals
Tarakamantram	A single mantram continuously chanted (to invoke a god or to attain victory)
Thali	The sacred thread tied around the neck of the bride during the marriage ceremony
Thiruneer	Holy ash
Thoranam	Decorations made of mango or palm leaves
Thumbai	White-coloured flowers
Thundu	A small piece of white cloth
Udukku	A small drum played to drive away evil spirits
Vaidyar	Indigenous medical practitioner
Vakil	Advocate
Varappu	A small bund made to arrest water seepage from one plot of the field to the other
Vathiyar	Teacher
Veshti	White cloth worn as a lower garment by men

Food items

Appalam	A round, deep-fried wafer, usually made of black gram
Cholam	A variety of grain
Chou-chou	A variety of vegetable
Ellu	Sesame
Kadalai	Groundnut
Kambu	Millet
Kanji	Porridge
Keerai	Leafy greens
Kollu	Horsegram
Kothavarangai	Country beans

Mixture	A fried snack
Nannari	Juice concentrate made from nannari roots
Pakoda	A snack made by frying gram flour mixed with onions, green chillies and spices
Paruppu	Lentils
Payasam	A sweet dish, usually made with milk
Payathamparuppu	Greengram
Peerkai	A vegetable belonging the gourd family
Puttu	Steamed rice flour and coconut, usually had as breakfast
Ragi	A cereal usually grown in semi-arid and hilly areas
Sukku coffee	Coffee prepared from dried ginger
Thenai	A type of millet grown in hilly areas
Thulasi	Basil leaves
Vadai	A fried snack
Zarda	Flavoured betel nut

Caste terms

Brahmin	The Hindu priestly caste, placed on top of the caste hierarchy
Chakkiliyar	An aboriginal agricultural community. Chakkiliyars work with leather, and are considered untouchables.
Gounder	A landowning caste Hindu community
Iyer	A community of Tamil Brahmins
Kudiyanavar	Caste Hindu communities
Melakkaran	Drummer
Mudaliyar	A landowning caste Hindu community
Nadar	A community, now involved in trade, located in the lower rungs of the caste Hindu hierarchy
Naicker	An agricultural community, located in the lower rungs of the caste Hindu hierarchy

Padayachi	An agricultural caste Hindu community
Pallar	An aboriginal agricultural community. Pallars are considered untouchables.
Parachi	A woman of the Parayar community
Para-vannar	The washerfolk community who work for the Parayars
Parayar	An aboriginal agricultural community. Parayars were forced to do menial jobs like burning the dead, and are considered untouchables.
Poosari	Priest (usually of non-Brahmin origin)
Reddiyar	A landowning caste Hindu community
Udayachi	A woman from the Udayar caste
Udayar	A landowning caste Hindu community
Valluva Pandaram	A priest from Valluvar community, the priestly class among the Scheduled castes
Vanniyar	The Padayachis choose to identify themselves as Vanniyars.
Vettiyan	A Vettiyan buries the dead among the Parayars.

Expressions

Aaya	Expression (addressing a woman) used to show affection
Atha	Mother
Ayyo	Expression used when one is shocked or hurt
Ayyo Sivane	Oh God!
Chandali	A derogatory expression, naming a person untouchable
Dei/di	Disrespectful/informal forms of address (Dei–Man; Di–Woman)
Eley/Ey	Ordering people with authority and also with disrespect

Endi/Enda/Ennadi	Disrespectful expressions of enquiry
Esaman	Respectful term used to address the employer or landlord
Kezhavi	Aged woman
Mottachi	Bald woman (derogatory usage)
Nondichi	Crippled woman (derogatory usage)
Paavi	Sinner
Pappa	Child
Sami	God
Saniyane	A curse word referring to the planet Saturn
Vanakkam	A respectful greeting

Kinship terms

Amma	Mother
Anna	Elder brother
Appa	Father
Appayi	Grandmother (father's mother)
Athai	Aunt
Ayya	Father
Chinnamma	Stepmother or mother's younger sister
Chithappa	Father's younger brother
Mama	Uncle (usually mother's brother)
Mami	Aunt (uncle's wife)
Periamma	Mother's elder sister
Periappa	Father's elder brother
Thambi	Younger brother
Thatha	Grandfather